Matilda

by

Mary Shelley

BΔNDΔNNΔ BOOKS   2013   SΔNTΔ BΔRBΔRΔ

Introduction copyright © 2013 Bandanna Books.
www.bandannabooks.com • ISBN 978-0-942208-49-8
Design by Joan Blake • Editing by Sasha Newborn

BANDANNA BOOKS

Don't Panic: Procrastinator's Guide to Writing an Effective Term Paper
The First Detective: 3 Stories. Edgar Allan Poe   **Gandhi on the** *Gita*
The Everlasting Gospel, William Blake   **Hadji Murad,** Leo Tolstoy
Dante & His Circle. Love sonnets   **Vita Nuova,** Dante on Beatrice
Ghazals of Ghalib   **The Gospel According to Tolstoy**
Mitos y Leyendas/Myths and Legends of Mexico. Bilingual
The Beechers Through the 19th Century   **First Person Intense**
Uncle Tom's Cabin, H.B, Stowe   **Aurora Leigh**, E.B. Browning
       Frankenstein, Mary Shelley   Matilda, Mary Shelley

TEACHING SUPPLEMENTS

(*Q & A, glossaries, critical comments*)
Areopagitica, John Milton   **Apology of Socrates, & The Crito,** Plato
      Leaves of Grass, Walt Whitman   **Sappho, The Poems**
Uncle Tom's Cabin, Harriet Beecher Stowe

SHAKESPEARE FOR DIRECTORS, PRODUCERS, ACTORS, WANNABEES

DIRECTOR'S PLAYBOOK SERIES. the elements of production:
storyboarding, auditions, staging diagrams, budget, publicity, costuming, set
      design, playbill, stage managing, glossary, customized actor scripts

Hamlet The Merchant of Venice   Twelfth Night   Taming of the Shrew
A Midsummer Night's Dream Romeo and Juliet As You Like It   Richard III
Henry V   Much Ado About Nothing   Macbeth   Othello

plus
7 Plays with Transgender Characters   Falstaff   Venus and Adonis

MUDBORN PRESS

First Person Intense   The Basement   Eight 2 Two
Italian for Opera Lovers   French for Food Lovers
Rockbottom (litmag)

CONTENTS

INTRODUCTION

Mary Shelley wrote *Matilda* not long after the phenomenal success of her first novel, *Frankenstein, The Modern Prometheus*. However, that publication did not carry her name until the second printing five years later.

She sent the manuscript of *Matilda* to her father, William Godwin, who refused to return it to her, probably because of the intimation of incestuous feelings by a father to a daughter. Whether this was autobiographically based or not, readers would assume the worst. Over a hundred years would pass before *Matilda* would reach the public.

Her parents, William Godwin and Mary Wollstonecraft, were famous radicals. Mary Wollstonecraft, an early feminist, died shortly after giving birth to Mary. Godwin did remarry, but his interests were with his equals rather than his daughter; he often entertained other leading writers and intellectuals, such as Charles Lamb, Coleridge, Hazlitt — and Percy Bysshe Shelley, whom she met when she was 14. At 16, the two of them eloped. On a stormy night on Lake Geneva, Dr. Polidori, Byron, and the Shelleys indulged in a contest to see who could come up with the scariest story — this was the era of the Gothic novel, vampires, and ghosts. And Mary Shelley had just lost her second child. Her contribution to the evening's entertainment was soon turned into the novel *Frankenstein*, which was an immediate sensation. Innovative in its storyline rather than its style, *Frankenstein* is sometimes touted as the first true science fiction novel.

The Shelleys lived together in various places in Europe for eight years, when Shelley died in a boating accident. Mary turned to writing novels to make her way.

True to the Romantic tradition, the short novel *Matilda* explored human emotions in their depths. Family tragedy, loss, incest, total withdrawal—these themes would have been influenced by the her depression following the loss of her children in early childhood. Only one child would reach adulthood.

This intimate story, and later novels were not to recapture the popular imagination as *Frankenstein* had. She would continue writing historical novels, romantic novels, a travel book, until she died at 54.

Though her social concerns remained, her issues did not coincide with her father's ideas. He is known as one of the first to articulate the doctrine of utilitarianism, and he wrote several novels, most notably *Caleb Williams*, which was written as a plea for social justice. She advocated cooperation rather than confrontation, social reform, vegetarianism, and, unlike her father, advocated for marriage—to which Shelley later agreed.

How much of Mary Shelley do we see in this short novel? We can only guess. She grew up during the last days of Napoleon, in an era of ferment, radical thinking, new possibilities for women, and a burgeoning literature of gushing emotion we now call the Romantic Era (some traces of it remain in our cultural life).

Text has been edited for the modern reader; the ebook version is interactive. Notes are at the end.

Sasha Newborn
February 2013

CHAPTER ONE

Florence. Nov. 9th, 1819

It is only four o'clock, but it is winter and the sun has already set: there are no clouds in the clear, frosty sky to reflect its slant beams, but the air itself is tinged with a slight roseate color which is again reflected on the snow that covers the ground. I live in a lone cottage on a solitary, wide heath; no voice of life reaches me. I see the desolate plain covered with white, save a few black patches that the noonday sun has made at the top of those sharp-pointed hillocks from which the snow, sliding as it fell, lay thinner than on the plain ground. A few birds are pecking at the hard ice that covers the pools—for the frost has been of long continuance.

I am in a strange state of mind. I am alone, quite alone, in the world—the blight of misfortune has passed over me and withered me. I know that I am about to die and I feel happy—joyous. I feel my pulse; it beats fast. I place my thin hand on my cheek, it burns; there is a slight, quick spirit within me which is now emitting its last sparks. I shall never see the snows of another winter—I do believe that I shall never again feel the vivifying warmth of another summer sun; and it is in this persuasion that I begin to write my tragic history. Perhaps a history such as mine had better die with me, but a feeling that I cannot define leads me on and I am too weak both in body and mind to resist the slightest impulse. While life was strong within me I thought indeed that there was a sacred horror in my tale that rendered it unfit for utterance, and now about to die I pollute its mystic terrors. It is as the wood of the Eumenides, none but the dying may enter; and Oedipus is about to die.

What am I writing? I must collect my thoughts. I do not know that any will peruse these pages except you, my friend, who will receive them at my death. I do not address them to you alone because it will give me pleasure to dwell upon our friendship in a way that would be needless if you alone read what I shall write. I shall relate my tale therefore as if I wrote for strangers.

You have often asked me the cause of my solitary life, my tears, and above all of my impenetrable and unkind silence. In life I dared not; in death I unveil the mystery. Others will toss these pages lightly over; to you, Woodville, kind, affectionate friend, they will be dear—the precious memorials of a heartbroken woman who, dying, is still warmed by gratitude towards you. Your tears will fall on the words that record my misfortunes; I know they will—and while I have life, I thank you for your sympathy.

But enough of this. I will begin my tale—it is my last task, and I hope I have strength sufficient to fulfill it. I record no crimes; my faults may easily be pardoned, for they proceeded not from evil motive but from want of judgment; and I believe few would say that they could, by a different conduct and superior wisdom, have avoided the misfortunes to which I am the victim. My fate has been governed by necessity, a hideous necessity. It required hands stronger than mine; stronger I do believe than any human force, to break the thick, adamantine chain that has bound me, once breathing nothing but joy, ever possessed by a warm love and delight in goodness—to misery only to be ended, and now about to be ended, in death. But I forget myself, my tale is yet untold. I will pause a few moments, wipe my dim eyes, and endeavor to lose the present obscure but heavy feeling of unhappiness in the more acute emotions of the past.

I was born in England. My father was a man of rank: he had lost his father early, and was educated by a weak mother with all the indulgence she thought due to a nobleman of wealth. He was sent to Eton and afterwards to college, and allowed from childhood the free use of large sums of money; thus enjoying from his earliest youth the independence which a boy with these advantages always acquires at a public school.

Under the influence of these circumstances, his passions found a deep soil wherein they might strike their root and flourish either as flowers or weeds as was their nature. By being always allowed to act for himself, his character became strongly and early marked and exhibited a various surface on which a quick-sighted observer might see the seeds of virtue and of misfortune. His careless extravagance, which made him squander immense sums of money to satisfy passing whims, which from their apparent energy he dignified with the name of passions, often displayed itself in unbounded generosity. Yet while he earnestly occupied himself about the wants of others, his own desires were gratified to their fullest extent. He gave his money, but none of his own wishes were sacrificed to his gifts; he gave his time, which he did not value, and his affections, which he was happy in any manner to have called into action.

I do not say that if his own desires had been put in competition with those of others that he would have displayed undue selfishness, but this trial was never made. He was nurtured in prosperity and attended by all its advantages; everyone loved him and wished to gratify him. He was ever employed in promoting the pleasures of his companions—but their pleasures were his; and if he bestowed more attention upon the feelings of others than is usual with schoolboys, it was because his social temper could never enjoy itself if every brow was not as free from care as his own.

While at school, emulation and his own natural abilities made him hold a conspicuous rank in the forms among his equals; at college he discarded books; he believed that he had other lessons to learn than those which they could teach him. He was now to enter into life and he was still young enough to consider study as a schoolboy shackle, employed merely to keep the unruly out of mischief but as having no real connection with life—whose wisdom of riding, gaming, etc., he considered with far deeper interest. So he quickly entered into all college follies, although his heart was too well molded to be contaminated by them—it might be light but it was never cold. He was a sincere and sympathizing friend, but he had met with none who, superior or equal to himself, could aid him in unfolding his mind, or make him seek for fresh stores of thought by exhausting the old ones. He felt himself superior in quickness of judgment to those around him; his talents, his rank and wealth made him the chief of his party, and in that station he rested not only contented but glorying, conceiving it to be the only ambition worthy for him to aim at in the world.

By a strange narrowness of ideas he viewed all the world in connection only as it was or was not related to his little society. He considered queer and out of fashion all opinions that were exploded by his circle of intimates, and he became at the same time dogmatic and yet fearful of not coinciding with the only sentiments he could consider orthodox. To the generality of spectators he appeared careless of censure, and with high disdain to throw aside all dependence on public prejudices—but at the same time he strode with a triumphant stride over the rest of the world. He cowered, with self-disguised lowliness, to his own party, and, although its chief, never dared express an opinion or a feeling until he was assured that it would meet with the approbation of his companions.

Yet he had one secret hidden from these dear friends, a secret he had nurtured from his earliest years, and, although he loved his fellow collegiates, he would not trust it to the delicacy or sympathy of any one among them. He loved. He feared that the intensity of his passion might become the subject of their ridicule, and he could not bear that they should blaspheme it by considering that trivial and transitory which he felt was the life of his life.

There was a gentleman of small fortune who lived near his family mansion who had three lovely daughters. The eldest was far the most beautiful, but her beauty was only an addition to her other qualities—her understanding was clear and strong, and her disposition angelically gentle. She and my father had been playmates from infancy. Diana, even in her childhood, had been a favorite with his mother; this partiality increased with the years of this beautiful and lively girl—and thus during his school and college vacations they were perpetually together. Novels, and all the various methods by which youth in civilized life are led to a knowledge of the existence of passions before they really feel them, had produced a strong effect on him, who was so peculiarly susceptible of every impression. At eleven years of age Diana was his favorite playmate, but he already talked the language of love. Although she was elder than he by nearly two years, the nature of her education made her more childish, at least in the knowledge and expression of feeling. She received his warm protestations with innocence, and returned them unknowing of what they meant. She had read no novels and associated only with her younger sisters—what could she know of the difference between love and friendship? And when the development of her understanding disclosed the true nature of this intercourse to her, her affections were already engaged to her friend, and all she feared was lest other attractions and fickleness might make him break his infant vows.

But they became every day more ardent and tender. It was a passion that had grown with his growth; it had become entwined with every faculty and every sentiment and only to be lost with life. None knew of their love except their own two hearts; yet although in all things else, and even in this, he dreaded the censure of his companions, for thus truly loving one inferior to him in fortune, nothing was ever able for a moment to shake his purpose of uniting himself to her as soon as he could muster the courage sufficient to meet those difficulties he was determined to surmount.

Diane was fully worthy of his deepest affection. There were few who could boast of so pure a heart, and so much real humbleness of soul joined to a firm reliance on her own integrity and a belief in that of others. She had from her birth lived a retired life. She had lost her mother when very young, but her father had devoted himself to the care of her education. He had many peculiar ideas which influenced the system he had adopted with regard to her;

she was well acquainted with the heroes of Greece and Rome, or with those of England who had lived some hundred years ago, while she was nearly ignorant of the passing events of the day. She had read few authors who had written during at least the last fifty years, but her reading with this exception was very extensive. Thus, although she appeared to be less initiated in the mysteries of life and society than he, her knowledge was of a deeper kind and laid on firmer foundations; and if even her beauty and sweetness had not fascinated him, her understanding would ever have held his in thrall. He looked up to her as his guide, and such was his adoration that he delighted to augment to his own mind the sense of inferiority with which she sometimes impressed him.

When he was nineteen his mother died. He left college on this event and, shaking off for a while his own friends, he retired to the neighborhood of his Diana and received all his consolation from her sweet voice and dearer caresses. This short separation from his companions gave him courage to assert his independence. He had a feeling that, however they might express ridicule of his intended marriage, they would not dare display it when it had taken place; therefore seeking the consent of his guardian, which with some difficulty he obtained, and of the father of his mistress which was more easily given, without acquainting anyone else of his intention, by the time he had attained his twentieth birthday he had become the husband of Diana.

He loved her with passion, and her tenderness had a charm for him that would not permit him to think of any but her. He invited some of his college friends to see him, but their frivolity disgusted him. Diana had torn the veil which had before kept him in his boyhood. He had become a man, and he was surprised how he could ever have joined in the cant words and ideas of his fellow collegiates, or how for a moment he had feared the censure of such as these. He discarded his old friendships not from fickleness but because they were indeed unworthy of him. Diana filled up all his heart. He felt as if by his union with her he had received a new and better soul. She was his monitor as he learned what were the true ends of life. It was through her beloved lessons that he cast off his old pursuits and gradually formed himself to become one among his fellow human beings, a distinguished member of society, a patriot, and an enlightened lover of truth and virtue. He loved her for her beauty and for her amiable disposition but he seemed to love her more for what he considered her superior wisdom. They studied, they rode together; they were never separate and seldom admitted a third to their society.

Thus my father, born in affluence, and always prosperous, climbed, without the difficulty and various disappointments that all human beings seem destined to encounter, to the very topmost pinnacle of happiness. Around him was sunshine. And clouds, whose shapes of beauty made the prospect divine, concealed from him the barren reality which lay hidden below them. From this dizzy point he was dashed at once as he unawares congratulated himself on his felicity. Fifteen months after their marriage I was born, and my mother died a few days after my birth.

A sister of my father was with him at this period. She was nearly fifteen years older than he, and was the offspring of a former marriage of his father. When the latter died, this sister was taken by her maternal relations; my father and she had seldom seen one another, and were quite unlike in disposition. This aunt, to whose care I was afterwards consigned, has often related to me the effect that this catastrophe had on my father's strong and susceptible character. From the moment of my mother's death until his departure, she never heard him utter a single word. Buried in the deepest melancholy, he took no notice of anyone; often for hours his eyes streamed tears or a more fearful gloom overpowered him. All outward things seemed to have lost their existence relative to him—and only one circumstance could in any degree recall him from his motionless and mute despair; he would never see me. He seemed insensible to the presence of anyone else, but if, as a trial to awaken his sensibility, my aunt brought me into the room he would instantly rush out with every symptom of fury and distraction. At the end of a month he suddenly quitted his house and, unattended by any servant, departed from that part of the country without by word or writing informing anyone of his intentions. My aunt was only relieved of her anxiety concerning his fate by a letter from him dated from Hamburg.

How often have I wept over that letter which, until I was sixteen, was the only relic I had to remind me of my parents.

> "Pardon me," it said, "for the uneasiness I have unavoidably given you: but while in that unhappy island, where everything breathes *her* spirit whom I have lost forever, a spell held me. It is broken. I have quitted England for many years, perhaps forever. But to convince you that selfish feeling does not entirely engross me I shall remain in this town until you have made by letter every arrangement that you judge necessary. When I leave this place, do not expect to hear from me: I must break all ties that at present exist. I shall become a wanderer, a miserable outcast—alone! alone!" In another part of the letter he mentioned me—"As for that unhappy little being whom I could not see, and hardly dare mention, I leave her under your protection. Take care of her and cherish her.. One day I may claim her at your hands; but futurity is dark; make the present happy to her."

My father remained three months at Hamburg; when he quitted it, he changed his name. My aunt could never discover that which he adopted and only by faint hints could conjecture that he had taken the road of Germany and Hungary to Turkey.

Thus this towering spirit, who had excited interest and high expectation in all who knew and could value him, became at once, as it were, extinct. He existed from this moment for himself only. His friends remembered him as a brilliant vision which would never again return to them. The memory of what he had been faded away as years passed; and he who before had been as a part of themselves and of their hopes was now no longer counted among the living.

CHAPTER TWO

I now come to my own story. During the early part of my life there is little to relate, and I will be brief; but I must be allowed to dwell a little on the years of my childhood, that it may be apparent how, when one hope failed, all life was to be a blank; and how, when the only affection I was permitted to cherish was blasted, my existence was extinguished with it.

I have said that my aunt was very unlike my father. I believe that, without the slightest tinge of a bad heart, she had the coldest that ever filled a human breast—it was totally incapable of any affection. She took me under her protection because she considered it her duty, but she had too long lived alone and undisturbed by the noise and prattle of children to allow that I should disturb her quiet. She had never been married, and for the last five years had lived perfectly alone on an estate that had descended to her through her mother, on the shores of Loch Lomond in Scotland. My father had expressed a wish in his letters that she should reside with me at his family mansion, which was situated in a beautiful country near Richmond in Yorkshire. She would not consent to this proposition, but, as soon as she had arranged the affairs which her brother's departure had caused to fall to her care, she quitted England and took me with her to her Scottish estate.

The care of me while a baby, and afterwards until I had reached my eighth year, devolved on a servant of my mother's who had accompanied us in our retirement for that purpose. I was placed in a remote part of the house, and only saw my aunt at stated hours. These occurred twice a day; once about noon she came to my nursery, and once after her dinner I was taken to her. She never caressed me, and seemed, all the time I stayed in the room, to fear that I shoud annoy her by some childish freak. My good nurse always schooled me with the greatest care before she ventured into the parlor—and the awe my aunt's cold looks and few constrained words inspired was so great that I seldom disgraced her lessons or was betrayed from the exemplary stillness which I was taught to observe during these short visits.

Under my good nurse's care, I ran wild about our park and the neighboring fields. The offspring of the deepest love, I displayed from my earliest years the greatest sensibility of disposition. I cannot say with what passion I loved every thing—even the inanimate objects that surrounded me. I believe that I bore an individual attachment to every tree in our park; every animal that inhabited it knew me, and I loved them. Their occasional deaths filled my infant heart with anguish. I cannot number the birds that I have saved during the long and severe winters of that climate; or the hares and rabbits that I have defended from the attacks of our dogs, or have nursed when accidentally wounded.

When I was seven years of age, my nurse left me. I now forget the cause of her departure, if indeed I ever knew it. She returned to England, and the bitter tears she shed at parting were the last I saw flow for love of me for many years. My grief was terrible: I had no friend but her in the whole world. By degrees, I became reconciled to solitude—but no one supplied her place in my affections. I lived in a desolate country where

> —there were none to praise
> And very few to love

It is true that I now saw a little more of my aunt, but she was in every way an unsocial being—and, to a timid child, she was as a plant beneath a thick covering of ice: I should cut my hands in endeavoring to get at it. So I was entirely thrown upon my own resources. The neighboring minister was engaged to give me lessons in reading, writing and French, but he was without family—and his manners, even to me, were always perfectly characteristic of the profession in the exercise of whose functions he chiefly shone, that of a schoolmaster. I sometimes strove to form friendships with the most attractive of the girls who inhabited the neighboring village; but I believe I should never have succeeded—even had not my aunt interposed her authority to prevent all intercourse between me and the peasantry. For she was fearful that I should acquire the Scottish accent and dialect; a little of it I had, although great pains were taken that my tongue should not disgrace my English origin.

As I grew older, my liberty increased with my desires, and my wanderings extended from our park to the neighboring country. Our house was situated on the shores of the lake and the lawn came down to the water's edge. I rambled amidst the wild scenery of this lovely country and became a complete mountaineer. I passed hours on the steep brow of a mountain that overhung a waterfall or rowed myself in a little skiff to one of the islands. I wandered forever about these lovely solitudes, gathering flower after flower.

> Ond' era pinta tutta la mia via
> where my pathway was full of color

singing as I might the wild melodies of the country, or occupied by pleasant daydreams. My greatest pleasure was the enjoyment of a serene sky amidst these verdant woods, yet I loved all the changes of Nature; and rain, and storm, and the beautiful clouds of heaven brought their delights with them. When rocked by the waves of the lake, my spirits rose in triumph as riders feel with pride the motion of their high-fed steeds.

But my pleasures arose from the contemplation of nature alone, I had no companion. My warm affections, finding no return from any other human heart, were forced to run waste on inanimate objects. Sometimes indeed I wept when my aunt received my caresses with repulsive coldness, and when I looked round and found none to love—but I quickly dried my tears. As I grew older, books in some degree supplied the place of human intercourse; the library of my aunt was very small. Shakespeare, Milton, Pope and Cowper were the strangely assorted poets of her collection; and, among the prose authors, a translation of Livy and Rollin's *Ancient History* were my chief favorites, although, as I emerged from childhood, I found others highly interesting which I had before neglected as dull.

When I was twelve years old, it occurred to my aunt that I ought to learn music; she herself played upon the harp. It was with great hesitation that she persuaded herself to undertake my instruction; yet, believing this accomplishment a necessary part of my education, and balancing the evils of this measure or of having someone in the house to instruct me, she submitted to the inconvenience. A harp was sent for, that my playing might not interfere with hers, and I began. She found me a docile and, when I had conquered the first rudiments, a very apt scholar. I had acquired in my harp a companion in rainy days—a sweet soother of my feelings when any untoward accident ruffled them. I often addressed it as my only friend; I could pour forth to it my hopes and loves, and I fancied that its sweet accents answered me. I have now mentioned all my studies.

I was a solitary being, and from my infant years, ever since my dear nurse left me, I had been a dreamer. I brought Rosalind and Miranda and the lady of Comus to life to be my companions, or on my isle acted over their parts, imagining myself to be in their situations. Then I wandered from the fancies of others and formed affections and intimacies with the aerial creations of my own brain—but, still clinging to reality, I gave a name to these conceptions and nursed them in the hope of realization.

I clung to the memory of my parents. My mother I should never see—she was dead—but the idea of my unhappy, wandering father was the idol of my imagination. I bestowed on him all my affections; there was a miniature of him that I gazed on continually. I copied his last letter and read it again and again. Sometimes it made me weep, and at others I repeated with transport those words—

"One day I may claim her at your hands"

—I was to be his consoler, his companion in after years. My favorite vision was that when I grew up I would leave my aunt, whose coldness lulled my conscience, and, disguised as a boy, I would seek my father through the world. My imagination hung upon the scene of recognition; his miniature, which I should continually wear exposed on my breast, would be the means—and I imagined the moment in my mind a thousand and a thousand times, perpetually varying the circumstances. Sometimes it would be in a desert, in a populous city, at a ball— we should perhaps meet in a vessel. And his first words constantly were, "My daughter, I love thee!" What ecstatic moments have I passed in these dreams! How many tears I have shed; how often have I laughed aloud.

This was my life for sixteen years. At fourteen and fifteen, I often thought that the time was come when I should commence my pilgrimage—which I had cheated my own mind into believing was my imperious duty. But a reluctance to quit my aunt, a remorse for the grief which, I could not conceal from myself, I should occasion her, forever withheld me. Sometimes when I had planned the next morning for my escape, a word of more than usual affection from her lips made me postpone my resolution. I reproached myself bitterly for what I called a culpable weakness; but this weakness returned upon me whenever the critical moment approached, and I never found courage to depart.

CHAPTER THREE

It was on my sixteenth birthday that my aunt received a letter from my father. I cannot describe the tumult of emotions that arose with in me as I read it. It was dated from London; he had returned! I could only relieve my transports by tears, tears of unmingled joy. He had returned, and he wrote to know whether my aunt would come to London or whether he should visit her in Scotland. How delicious to me were the words of his letter that concerned me.

> "I cannot tell you," it said, "how ardently I desire to see my Matilda. I look on her as the creature who will form the happiness of my future life. She is all that exists on Earth that interests me. I can hardly prevent myself from hastening immediately to you, but I am necessarily detained a week, and I write because if you come here I may see you somewhat sooner."

I read these words with devouring eyes; I kissed them, wept over them and exclaimed, "He will love me!"

My aunt would not undertake so long a journey, and in a fortnight we had another letter from my father. It was dated from Edinburgh. He wrote that he should be with us in three days.

> "As I approach, my desire of seeing you," he said, "becomes more and more ardent, and I feel that the moment when I should first clasp you in my arms would be the happiest of my life."

How irksome were these days to me! All sleep and appetite fled from me; I could only read and re-read his letter, and in the solitude of the woods imagine the moment of our meeting. On the eve of the third day I retired early to my room; I could not sleep, but paced all night about my chamber, and, as you may in Scotland at midsummer, I watched the crimson track of the sun as it almost skirted the northern horizon. At daybreak I hastened to the woods; the hours passed on while I indulged in wild dreams that gave wings to the slothful steps of time, and beguiled my eager impatience.

My father was expected at noon, but when I wished to return to meet him, I found that I had lost my way. It seemed that in every attempt to find it, I only became more involved in the intricacies of the woods, and the trees hid all trace by which I might be guided. I grew impatient, I wept, and wrung my hands, but still I could not discover my path.

It was past two o'clock when, by a sudden turn, I found myself close to the lake near a cove where a little skiff was moored—it was not far from our house, and I saw my father and aunt walking on the lawn. I jumped into the boat and, well accustomed to such feats, I pushed it from the shore, and exerted all my strength to row swiftly across. As I came, dressed in white, covered only by my tartan rachan, my hair streaming on my shoulders, and shooting across with greater speed than it could be supposed I could give to my boat—my father has often told me that I looked more like a spirit than a human maid. I approached the shore, my father held the boat, I leaped lightly out, and in a moment was in his arms.

And now I began to live. All around me was changed from a dull uniformity to the brightest scene of joy and delight. The happiness I enjoyed in the company of my father far exceeded my sanguine expectations. We were forever together, and the subjects of our conversations were inexhaustible. He had passed the sixteen years of absence among nations nearly unknown to Europe; he had wandered through Persia, Arabia, and the north of India, and had penetrated among the habitations of the natives with a freedom permitted to few Europeans. His relations of their manners, his anecdotes and descriptions of scenery whiled away delicious hours, when we were tired of talking of our own plans of future life.

The voice of affection was so new to me that I hung with delight upon his words when he told me what he had felt concerning me during these long years of apparent forgetfulness.

"At first," said he, "I could not bear to think of my poor little girl; but afterwards, as grief wore off and hope again revisited me, I could only turn to her, and amidst cities and deserts her little fairy form, such as I imagined it, forever flitted before me. The northern breeze as it refreshed me was sweeter and more balmy, for it seemed to carry some of your spirit along with it. I often thought that I would instantly return and take you along with me to some fertile island where we should live at peace forever. As I returned, my fervent hopes were dashed by so many fears; my impatience became in the highest degree painful. I dared not think that the sun should shine and the moon rise on your living form but on your grave. But, no. It is not so; I have my Matilda, my consolation, and my hope."

My father was very little changed from what he described himself to be before his misfortunes. It is intercourse with civilized society; it is the disappointment of cherished hopes, the falsehood of friends, or the perpetual clash of mean passions that changes the heart and damps the ardor of youthful feelings. Lonely wanderings in a wild country among people of simple or savage manners may inure the body, but will not tame the soul, or extinguish the ardor and freshness of feeling incident to youth. The burning sun of India, and the freedom from all restraint had rather increased the energy of his character. Before, he bowed under. Now he was impatient of any censure except that of his own mind. He had seen so many customs and witnessed so great a variety of moral creeds that he had been obliged to form an independent one for himself, which had no relation to the peculiar notions of any one country. His early prejudices, of course, influenced his judgment in the formation of his principles—and some raw college ideas were strangely mingled with the deepest deductions of his penetrating mind.

The vacuity his heart endured of any deep interest in life during his long absence from his native country had had a singular effect upon his ideas. There was a curious feeling of unreality attached by him to his foreign life in comparison with the years of his youth. All the time he had passed out of England was as a dream, and all the interest of his soul, all his affections belonged to events which had happened and persons who had existed sixteen years before. It was strange when you heard him talk to see how he passed over this lapse of time as a night of visions, while the remembrances of his youth, standing separate as they did from his after life, had lost none of their vigor. He talked of my mother as if she had lived but a few weeks before— not that he expressed poignant grief, but his description of her person, and his relation of all anecdotes connected with her was thus fervent and vivid.

In all this there was a strangeness that attracted and enchanted me. He was, as it were, now awakened from his long, visionary sleep, and he felt somewhat like one of the seven sleepers, or like Noujahad, in that sweet imitation of an Eastern tale. Diana was gone; his friends were changed or dead; and now on his awakening I was all that he had to love on Earth.

How dear to me were the waters, and mountains, and woods of Loch Lomond now that I had so beloved a companion for my rambles. I visited with my father every delightful spot, either on the islands, or by the side of the tree-sheltered waterfalls— every shady path, or dingle entangled with underwood and fern. My ideas were enlarged by his conversation. I felt as if I were recreated and had about me all the freshness and life of a new being. I was, as it were, transported since his arrival from a narrow spot of Earth into a universe boundless to the imagination and the understanding. My life had been before as a pleasing country rill, never destined to leave its native fields, but, when its task was fulfilled, quietly to be absorbed, and leave no trace. Now it seemed to me to be as a various river flowing through a fertile and lovely landscape, ever changing and ever beautiful. Alas! I knew not the desert it was about to reach, the rocks that would tear its waters, and the hideous scene that would be reflected in a more distorted manner in its waves. Life was then brilliant; I began to learn to hope and what brings a more bitter despair to the heart than hope destroyed?

Is it not strange that grief should quickly follow so divine a happiness? I drank of an enchanted cup, but gall was at the bottom of its long-drawn sweetness. My heart was full of deep affection, but it was calm from its very depth and fullness. I had no idea that misery could arise from love, and this lesson that all at last must learn was taught me in a manner few are obliged to receive. I lament now, I must ever lament, those short months of Paradisiacal bliss; I disobeyed no command, I ate no apple, and yet I was ruthlessly driven from it. Alas, my companion did, and I was precipitated in his fall. But I wander from my relation—let woe come at its appointed time; I may at this stage of my story still talk of happiness.

Three months passed away in this delightful intercourse, when my aunt fell ill. I passed a whole month in her chamber nursing her, but her disease was mortal and she died, leaving me for some time inconsolable. Death is so dreadful to the living; the chains of habit are so strong, even when affection does not link them, that the heart must be agonized when they break. But my father was beside me to console me and to drive away bitter memories by bright hopes; I thought that it was sweet to grieve that he might dry my tears.

Then again, he distracted my thoughts from my sorrow by comparing it with his despair when he lost my mother. Even at that time I shuddered at the picture he drew of his passions. He had the imagination of a poet, and when he described the whirlwind that then tore his feelings he gave his words the impress of life so vividly that I believed while I trembled. I wondered how he could ever again have entered into the offices of life after his wild thoughts seemed to have given him affinity with the unearthly. While he spoke, so tremendous were the ideas which he conveyed that it appeared as if the human heart were far too bounded for their conception. His feelings seemed better fitted for a spirit whose habitation is the earthquake and the volcano than for one confined to a mortal body and human lineaments. But these were merely memories; he was changed since then. He was now all love, all softness—and when I raised my eyes in wonder at him as he spoke, the smile on his lips told me that his heart was possessed by the gentlest passions.

Two months after my aunt's death we removed to London, where I was led by my father to attend to deeper studies than had before occupied me. My improvement was his delight; he was with me during all my studies and assisted or joined with me in every lesson. We saw a great deal of society, and no day passed that my father did not endeavor to embellish by some new enjoyment. The tender attachment that he bore me, and the love and veneration with which I returned it, cast a charm over every moment. The hours were slow, for each minute was employed; we lived more in one week than many do in the course of several months, and the variety and novelty of our pleasures gave zest to each.

We perpetually made excursions together. And whether it was to visit beautiful scenery, or to see fine pictures, or sometimes for no object but to seek amusement as it might chance to arise, I was always happy when near my father. It was a subject of regret to me whenever we were joined by a third person, yet, if I turned with a disturbed look towards my father, his eyes fixed on me and beaming with tenderness instantly restored joy to my heart. Oh, hours of intense delight! Short as they were, they are made as long to me as a whole life when looked back upon through the mist of grief that rose immediately after as if to shut them from my view. Alas! they were the last of happiness that I ever enjoyed; a few, a very few weeks and all was destroyed. Like Psyche, I lived for awhile in an enchanted palace, amidst scents, and music, and every luxurious delight, when suddenly I was left on a barren rock; a wide ocean of despair rolled around me—above all was black, and my eyes closed while I still inhabited a universal death. Still I would not hurry on; I would pause forever on the recollections of these happy weeks; I would repeat every word—and how many do I remember—record every enchantment of the fairy habitation. But, no, my tale must not pause; it must be as rapid as was my fate—I can only describe in short although strong expressions my precipitate and irremediable change from happiness to despair.

CHAPTER FOUR

Among our most assiduous visitors was a young man of rank, well informed, and agreeable in his person. After we had spent a few weeks in London, his attentions towards me became marked and his visits more frequent. I was too much taken up by my own occupations and feelings to attend much to this, and then indeed I hardly noticed more than the bare surface of events as they passed around me—but I now remember that my father was restless and uneasy whenever this person visited us, and when we talked together he watched us with the greatest apparent anxiety, although he himself maintained a profound silence. At length these obnoxious visits suddenly ceased altogether, but from that moment I must date the change of my father: a change that to remember makes me shudder and then filled me with the deepest grief. There were no degrees which could break my fall from happiness to misery; it was as the stroke of lightning—sudden and entire. Alas! I now met frowns where before I had been welcomed only with smiles: he, my beloved father, shunned me, and either treated me with harshness or a more heartbreaking coldness. We took no more sweet counsel together; and when I tried to win him again to me, his anger, and the terrible emotions that he exhibited drove me to silence and tears.

And this was sudden. The day before, we had passed alone together in this country; I remember we had talked of future travels that we should undertake together. There was an eager delight in our tones and gestures that could only spring from deep and mutual love joined to the most unrestrained confidence; and now the next day, the next hour, I saw his brows contracted, his eyes fixed in sullen fierceness on the ground, and his voice so gentle and so dear made me shiver when he addressed me. Often, when my wandering fancy brought by its various images now consolation and now aggravation of grief to my heart, I have compared myself to Proserpine who was gaily and heedlessly gathering flowers on the sweet plain of Enna, when the King of Hell snatched her to the abodes of death and misery. Alas! I who so lately knew of nothing but the joy of life, who had slept only to dream sweet dreams and awoke to incomparable happiness, I now passed my days and nights in tears. I who sought and had found joy in the love-breathing countenance of my father, now, when I dared fix on him a supplicating look, it was ever answered by an angry frown. I dared not speak to him; and when sometimes I had worked up courage to meet him and to ask an explanation, one glance at his face, where a chaos of mightily passion seemed forever struggling, made me tremble and shrink to silence. I was dashed down from Heaven to Earth as a silly sparrow when pounced on by a hawk; my eyes swam and my head was bewildered by the sudden apparition of grief. Day after day passed, marked only by my complaints and my tears; often I lifted my soul in vain prayer for a softer descent from joy to woe—or if that were denied me that I might be allowed to die, and fade forever under the cruel blast that swept over me,

> —for what should I do here,
> Like a decaying flower, still withering
> Under his bitter words, whose kindly heat
> Should give my poor heart life?

Sometimes I said to myself, this is an enchantment, and I must strive against it. My father is blinded by some malignant vision which I must remove. And then, like David, I would try music to win the evil spirit from him; and once while singing I lifted my eyes towards him and saw his fixed on me and filled with tears; all his muscles seemed relaxed to softness. I sprung towards him with a cry of joy and would have thrown myself into his arms, but he pushed me roughly from him and left me. And even from this slight incident he contracted fresh gloom and an additional severity of manner.

There are many incidents that I might relate which showed

the diseased yet incomprehensible state of his mind; but I will mention one that occurred while we were in company with several other persons. On this occasion I chanced to say that I thought *Myrrha* the best of Alfieri's tragedies; as I said this, I chanced to cast my eyes on my father and met his. For the first time, the expression of those beloved eyes pleased me, and I saw with fear that his whole frame shook with some concealed emotion that, in spite of his efforts, half conquered him. As this tempest faded from his soul he became melancholy and silent.

Every day some new scene occurred and displayed in him a mind working as if with an unknown horror that now he could master, but which at times threatened to overturn his reason, and to throw the bright seat of his intelligence into a perpetual chaos.

I will not dwell longer than I need on these disastrous circumstances. I might waste days in describing how anxiously I watched every change of fleeting circumstance that promised better days, and with what despair I found that each effort of mine aggravated his seeming madness. To tell all my grief, I might as well attempt to count the tears that have fallen from these eyes, or every sigh that has torn my heart. I will be brief for there is in all this a horror that will not bear many words, and I sink almost a second time to death while I recall these sad scenes to my memory. Oh, my beloved father! Indeed you made me miserable beyond all words, but how truly did I even then forgive you, and how entirely did you possess my whole heart while I endeavored, as a rainbow gleams upon a cataract, to soften your tremendous sorrows.

Thus did change come about. I seem perhaps to have dashed too suddenly into the description, but thus suddenly did it happen. In one sentence I have passed from the idea of unspeakable happiness to that of unspeakable grief, but they were this closely linked together. We had remained five months in London—three of joy and two of sorrow. My father and I were now seldom alone, or, if we were, he generally kept silence, with his eyes fixed on the ground—the dark full orbs in which before I delighted to read all sweet and gentle feeling shadowed from my sight by their lids and the long lashes that fringed them. When we were in company he affected gaiety, but I wept to hear his hollow laugh—begun by an empty smile and often ending in a bitter sneer such as never before this fatal period had wrinkled his lips. When others were there he often spoke to me and his eyes perpetually followed my slightest motion. His accents whenever he addressed me were cold and constrained, although his voice would tremble when he perceived that my full heart choked the answer to words proffered with a mien yet new to me.

But days of peaceful melancholy were of rare occurrence. They were often broken in on by gusts of passion that drove me as a weak boat on a stormy sea to seek a cove for shelter; but the winds blew from my native harbor and I was cast far, far out, until, shattered, I perished when the tempest had passed and the sea was apparently calm. I do not know that I can describe his emotions: sometimes he only betrayed them by a word or gesture, and then retired to his chamber—and I crept as near it as I dared and listened with fear to every sound, yet still more dreading a sudden silence—dreading I knew not what, but ever full of fear.

It was after one tremendous day when his eyes had glared on me like lightning—and his voice sharp and broken seemed unable to express the extent of his emotion—that in the evening when I was alone he joined me with a calm countenance, and, not noticing my tears which I quickly dried when he approached, told me that in three days he intended to remove with me to his estate in Yorkshire, and, bidding me prepare, left me hastily as if afraid of being questioned.

This determination on his part indeed surprised me. This estate was that which he had inhabited in his childhood and near which my mother resided while a girl; this was the scene of their youthful loves and where they had lived after their marriage. In happier days my father had often told me that, however he might appear weaned from his widow sorrow, and free from bitter recollections elsewhere, yet he would never dare visit the spot where he had enjoyed her society or trust himself to see the rooms that so many years ago they had inhabited together— her favorite walks and the gardens, the flowers of which she had delighted to cultivate. And now, while he suffered intense misery, he determined to plunge into still more intense, and strove for greater emotion than that which already tore him. I was perplexed, and most anxious to know what this portended. Ah, what could it portend but ruin?

I saw little of my father during this interval, but he appeared calmer, although not less unhappy than before. On the morning of the third day, he informed me that he had determined to go to Yorkshire first alone, and that I should follow him in a fortnight unless I heard anything from him in the meantime that should contradict this command. He departed the same day, and four days afterwards I received a letter from his steward telling me in his name to join him with as little delay as possible. After traveling day and night I arrived with an anxious, yet a hoping heart, for why should he send for me if it were only to avoid me and to treat me with the apparent aversion that he had in London?

I met him at the distance of thirty miles from our mansion. His demeanor was sad; for a moment he appeared glad to see me and then checked himself as if unwilling to betray his feelings. He was silent during our ride, yet his manner was kinder than before and I thought I saw a softness in his eyes that gave me hope.

When we arrived, after a little rest, he led me over the house and pointed out to me the rooms which my mother had inhabited. Although more than sixteen years had passed since her death, nothing had been changed; her workbox, her writing desk were still there and in her room a book lay open on the table as she had left it. My father pointed out these circumstances with a serious and unaltered mien, only now and then fixing his deep and liquid eyes upon me. There was something strange and awful in his look that overcame me, and, in spite of myself,

I wept—nor did he attempt to console me, but I saw his lips quiver and the muscles of his face seemed convulsed.

We walked together in the gardens and in the evening when I would have retired, he asked me to stay and read to him; and first said, "When I was last here your mother read Dante to me; you shall go on where she left off."

And then in a moment he said, "No, that must not be; you must not read Dante. Do you choose a book." I took up Spenser and read the descent of Sir Guyon to the halls of Avarice; while he listened, his eyes fixed on me in sad, profound silence.

I heard the next morning from the steward that, upon his arrival, my father had been in a most terrible state of mind—he had passed the first night in the garden lying on the damp grass; he did not sleep but groaned perpetually.

"Alas!" said the old man who gave me this account with tears in his eyes, "it wrings my heart to see my lord in this state. When I heard that he was coming down here with you, my young lady, I thought we should have the happy days over again that we enjoyed during the short life of my lady your mother. But that would be too much happiness for us poor creatures born to tears—and that was why she was taken from us so soon; she was too beautiful and good for us. It was a happy day, as we all thought, when my lord married her. I knew her when she was a child and many a good turn has she done for me in my old lady's time. You are like her, although there is more of my lord in you. But has he been thus ever since his return? All my joy turned to sorrow when I first beheld him with that melancholy countenance enter these doors as it were the day after my lady's funeral. He seemed to recover himself a little after he had bidden me write to you—but still it is a woeful thing to see him so unhappy."

These were the feelings of an old, faithful servant—what must be those of an affectionate daughter? Alas! Even then my heart was almost broken.

We spent two months together in this house. My father spent the greater part of his time with me; he accompanied me in my walks, listened to my music, and leaned over me as I read or painted. When he conversed with me his manner was cold and constrained. Only his eyes seemed to speak, and, as he turned their black, full luster towards me, they expressed a living sadness. There was something in those dark deep orbs so liquid and intense that even in happiness I could never meet their full gaze that mine did not overflow. Yet it was with sweet tears; now there was a depth of affliction in their gentle appeal that rent my heart with sympathy; they seemed to desire peace for me; for himself, a heart patient to suffer; a craving for sympathy, yet a perpetual self denial. It was only when he was absent from me that his passion subdued him—that he clinched his hands— knit his bows—and with haggard looks called for death to his despair, raving wildly, until exhausted he sank down, nor was revived until I joined him.

While we were in London, there was a harshness and sullenness in his sorrow which had now entirely disappeared. There, I shrunk and fled from him; now I only wished to be with him that I might soothe him to peace. When he was silent. I tried to divert him, and when sometimes I stole to him during the energy of his passion, I wept, but did not desire to leave him. Yet he suffered fearful agony. During the day, he was more calm, but at night, when I could not be with him, he seemed to give the reins to his grief. He often passed his nights either on the floor in my mother's room, or in the garden; and when in the morning he saw me view with poignant grief his exhausted frame, and his person languid almost to death with watching, he wept. But during all this time, he spoke no word by which I might guess the cause of his unhappiness. If I ventured to enquire, he would either leave me or press his finger on his lips, and with a deprecating look that I could not resist, turn away. If I wept, he would gaze on me in silence but he was no longer harsh and although he repulsed every caress, yet it was with gentleness.

He seemed to cherish a mild grief and softer emotions, although sad, as a relief from despair. He contrived in many ways to nurse his melancholy as an antidote to wilder passion.

He perpetually frequented the walks that had been favorites with him when he and my mother wandered together talking of love and happiness; he collected every relic that remained of her and always sat opposite her picture which hung in the room, fixing on it a look of sad despair—and all this was done in a mystic and awful silence. If his passion subdued him, he locked himself in his room; and at night when he wandered restlessly about the house, it was when every other creature slept.

It may easily be imagined that I wearied myself with conjecture to guess the cause of his sorrow. The solution that seemed to me the most probable was that, during his residence in London, he had fallen in love with some unworthy person, and that his passion mastered him although he would not gratify it. He loved me too well to sacrifice me to this inclination, and so he had now visited this house that, by reviving the memory of my mother whom he so passionately adored, he might weaken the present impression. This was possible; but it was a mere conjecture, unfounded on any fact. Could there be guilt in it? He was too upright and noble to do anything that his conscience would not approve. I did not yet know of the crime there may be in involuntary feeling, and therefore ascribed his tumultuous starts and gloomy looks wholly to the struggles of his mind and not any as they were partly due to the worst fiend of all—remorse.

But still do I flatter myself that this would have passed away. His paroxysms of passion were terrific, but his soul bore him through them triumphant, though almost destroyed by victory. But the day would finally have been won had not I—foolish and presumptuous wretch!—hurried him on until there was no recall, no hope. My rashness gave the victory in this dreadful fight to the enemy who triumphed over him as he lay fallen and vanquished. I! I alone was the cause of his defeat, and justly did I pay the fearful penalty. I said to myself, let him receive sympathy and these struggles will cease. Let him confide his misery to another heart and half the weight of it will be lightened. I will win him to me; he shall not deny his grief to me. And when I know his secret, then will I pour a balm into his soul and again I shall enjoy the ravishing delight of beholding his smile, and of again seeing his eyes beam, if not with pleasure, at least with gentle love and thankfulness. This will do, I said.

Half accomplished; I gained his secret and we were both lost forever.

CHAPTER FIVE

Nearly a year had passed since my father's return, and the seasons had almost finished their round. It was now the end of May; the woods were clothed in their freshest verdure, plus the sweet smell of the new-mown grass in the fields. I thought that the balmy air and the lovely face of Nature might aid me in inspiring him with mild sensations, and give him gentle feelings of peace and love preparatory to the confidence I determined to win from him.

I chose therefore the evening of one of these days for my attempt. I invited him to walk with me, and led him to a neighboring wood of beech trees whose light shade shielded us from the slant and dazzling beams of the descending sun. After walking for some time in silence I seated myself with him on a mossy hillock. It is strange, but even now I seem to see the spot—the slim and smooth trunks were, many of them, wound round by ivy whose shining leaves of the darkest green contrasted with the white bark and the light leaves of the young sprouts of beech that grew from their parent trunks. The short grass was mingled with moss and was partly covered by the dead leaves of the last autumn that, driven by the winds, had here and there collected in little hillocks. There were a few moss-grown stumps about. The leaves were gently moved by the breeze and through their green canopy you could see the bright blue sky. As evening came on, the distant trunks were reddened by the sun and the wind died entirely away, while a few birds flew past us to their evening rest.

Well, it was here we sat together, and when you hear all that passed—all that was terrible tore our souls even in this placid spot, which but for strange passions might have been a paradise to us—you will not wonder that I remember it as I looked on it that its calm might give me calm, and inspire me not only with courage but with persuasive words. I saw all these things and in a vacant manner noted them in my mind while I endeavored to arrange my thoughts in fitting order for my attempt. My heart beat fast as I worked myself up to speak to him, for I was determined not to be repulsed, but I trembled to imagine what effect my words might have on him; at length, with much hesitation I began:

"Your kindness to me, my dearest father, and the affection—the excessive affection—that you had for me when you first returned will, I hope, excuse me in your eyes that I dare speak to you—although with the tender affection of a daughter, yet also with the freedom of a friend and equal. But pardon me, I entreat you and listen to me. Do not turn away from me; do not be impatient. You may easily intimidate me into silence, but my heart is bursting, nor can I willingly consent to endure for one moment longer the agony of incertitude which for the last four months has been my portion.

"Listen to me, dearest friend, and permit me to gain your confidence. Are the happy days of mutual love which have passed to be to me as a dream never to return? Alas! You have a secret grief that destroys us both. But you must permit me to win this secret from you. Tell me, can I do nothing? You well know that on the whole Earth there is no sacrifice that I would not make, no labor that I would not undergo with the mere hope that I might bring you ease. But if no effort on my part can contribute to your happiness, let me at least know your sorrow, and surely my earnest love and deep sympathy must soothe your despair.

"I fear that I speak in a constrained manner. My heart is overflowing with the ardent desire I have of bringing calm once more to your thoughts and looks—but I fear to aggravate your grief, or to raise that in you which is death to me—anger and distaste. Do not then continue to fix your eyes on the earth; raise them on me, for I can read your soul in them. Speak to me, and pardon my presumption. Alas! I am a most unhappy creature!"

I was breathless with emotion, and I paused, fixing my earnest eyes on my father, after I had dashed away the intrusive tears that dimmed them. He did not raise his, but after a short silence, he replied to me in a low voice: "You are indeed presumptuous, Matilda, presumptuous and very rash. In the heart of one like me, there are secret thoughts working, and secret tortures which you ought not to seek to discover. I cannot tell you how it adds to my grief to know that I am the cause of uneasiness to you; but this will pass away, and I hope that soon we shall be as we were a few months ago. Restrain your impatience or you may mar what you attempt to alleviate. Do not again speak to me in this strain; but wait in submissive patience in the event of what is passing around you."

"Oh, yes!" I passionately replied, "I will be very patient; I will not be rash or presumptuous. I will see the agonies, and tears, and despair of my father, my only friend, my hope, my shelter, I will see it all with folded arms and downcast eyes. You do not treat me with candor. It is not true what you say; this will not soon pass away—it will last forever if you deign not to speak to me, to admit my consolations.

"Dearest, dearest father, pity me and pardon me. I entreat you do not drive me to despair; indeed I must not be repulsed. There is one thing that which, although it may torture me to know, yet that you must tell me. I demand, and most solemnly I demand if in any way I am the cause of your unhappiness. Do you not see my tears which I in vain strive against. You hear unmoved my voice broken by sobs. Feel how my hand trembles— my whole heart is in the words I speak, and you must not try to silence me by mere words barren of meaning. The agony of my doubt hurries me on, and you must reply. I beseech you; by your former love for me now lost, I ask you to answer this one question. Am I the cause of your grief?"

He raised his eyes from the ground, but still turning them away from me, said: "Besought by that plea I will answer your rash question. Yes, you are the sole, the agonizing cause of all I suffer, of all I must suffer until I die. Now, beware! Be silent! Do not urge me to your destruction. I am struck by the storm, rooted up, laid waste: but you can stand against it; you are young and your passions are at peace. One word I might speak and then you would be implicated in my destruction—yet that word is hovering on my lips. Oh! There is a fearful chasm; but I adjure you to beware!"

"Ah, dearest friend!" I cried, "Do not fear! Speak that word; it will bring peace, not death. If there is a chasm, our mutual love will give us wings to pass it, and we shall find flowers, and verdure, and delight on the other side." I threw myself at his feet, and took his hand, "Yes, speak, and we shall be happy; there will no longer be doubt, no dreadful uncertainty. Trust me, my affection will soothe your sorrow; speak that word and all danger will be past, and we shall love each other as before, and forever."

He snatched his hand from me, and rose in violent disorder: "What do you mean? You know not what you mean. Why do you bring me out, and torture me, and tempt me, and kill me—much happier would it be for you and me if in your frantic curiosity you tore my heart from my breast and tried to read its secrets in it as its life's blood was dropping from it. Thus you may console me by reducing me to nothing—but your words I cannot bear. Soon they will make me mad, quite mad, and then I shall utter strange words, and you will believe them, and we shall both be lost forever. I tell you I am on the very verge of insanity. Why, cruel girl, do you drive me on? You will repent and I shall die."

When I repeat his words I wonder at my pertinacious folly; I hardly know what feelings resistlessly impelled me. I believe it was that coming out with a determination not to be repulsed, I went right forward to my object without well weighing his replies. I was led by passion, and drew him with frantic heedlessness into the abyss that he so fearfully avoided. I replied to his terrific words: "You fill me with fear, it is true, dearest father, but you only confirm my resolution to put an end to this state of doubt. I will not be put off thus. Do you think that I can live thus fearfully from day to day—the sword in my heart yet kept from its mortal wound by a hair—a word! I demand that dreadful word; though it be as a flash of lightning to destroy me, speak it.

"Alas! Alas! What am I become? But a few months have elapsed since I believed that I was all the world to you and that there was no happiness or grief for you on Earth unshared by your Matilda—your child. That happy time is no longer, and what I most dreaded in this world is come upon me. In the despair of my heart I see what you cannot conceal. You no longer love me. I adjure you, my father, has not an unnatural passion seized upon your heart? Am I not the most miserable worm that crawls? Do I not embrace your knees, and you most cruelly repulse me? I know it—I see it—you hate me!"

I was transported by violent emotion, and rising from his feet, at which I had thrown myself, I leaned against a tree, wildly raising my eyes to heaven.

He began to answer with violence: "Yes, yes, I hate you! You are my bane, my poison, my disgust! Oh! No!"

And then his manner changed, and, fixing his eyes on me with an expression that convulsed every nerve and member of my frame, "You are none of all these; you are my light, my only one, my life. My daughter, I love you!" The last words died away in a hoarse whisper, but I heard them and sank on the ground, covering my face and almost dead with excess of sickness and fear. A cold perspiration covered my forehead and I shivered in every limb. But he continued, clasping his hands with a frantic gesture:

"Now I have dashed from the top of the rock to the bottom! Now I have precipitated myself down the fearful chasm. The danger is over; she is alive! Oh, Matilda, lift up those dear eyes in the light of which I live. Let me hear the sweet tones of your beloved voice in peace and calm. Monster as I am, you are still, as you ever were, lovely, beautiful beyond expression. What I have become since this last moment I know not; perhaps I am changed in mien as the fallen archangel. I do believe I am for I have surely a new soul within me, and my blood riots through my veins: I am burnt up with fever. But these are precious moments. Devil as I am become, yet that is my Matilda before me whom I love as one was never before loved. And she knows it now. She listens to these words which I thought, fool as I was, would blast her to death. Come, come, the worst is past. No more grief, tears or despair—were not those the words you uttered? We have leapt the chasm I told you of, and now, mark me, Matilda, we are to find flowers, and verdure and delight, or is it hell, and fire, and tortures? Oh! Beloved One, I am borne away; I can no longer sustain myself; surely this is death that is coming. Let me lay my head near your heart; let me die in your arms!" He sank to the earth fainting, while I, nearly as lifeless, gazed on him in despair.

Yes, it was despair I felt. For the first time, that phantom seized me—the first and only time, for it has never since left me. After the first moments of speechless agony, I felt its fangs on my heart. I tore my hair; I raved aloud. At one moment in pity for his sufferings, I would have clasped my father in my arms; and then starting back with horror I spurned him with my foot; I felt as if stung by a serpent, as if scourged by a whip of scorpions which drove me. Ah! Whither—whither?

Well, this could not last. One idea rushed on my mind. Never, never may I speak to him again. As this terrible conviction came upon me it melted my soul to tenderness and love—I gazed on him as to take my last farewell.

He lay insensible, his eyes closed and his cheeks deathly pale. Above, the leaves of the beech wood cast a flickering shadow on his face, and waved in mournful melody over him—I saw all these things and said, "Aye, this is his grave!" And then I wept aloud, and raised my eyes to leaven to entreat for a respite to my despair, and an alleviation for his unnatural suffering. The tears that gushed in a warm and healing stream from my eyes relieved the burden that oppressed my heart almost to madness. I wept for a long time until I saw him about to revive, when my horror and misery again recurred, and the tide of my sensations rolled back to their former channel. With a terror I could not restrain,

I sprang up and fled, with winged speed, along the paths of the wood and across the fields until, nearly dead, I reached our house, and just ordering the servants to seek my father at the spot I indicated, I shut myself up in my own room.

CHAPTER SIX

My chamber was in a retired part of the house, and looked upon the garden. so that no sound of the other inhabitants could reach it; and here in perfect solitude I wept for several hours. When a servant came to ask me if I would take food, I learned from him that my father had returned and was apparently well, and this relieved me from a load of anxiety, yet I did not cease to weep bitterly.

At first, as the memory of former happiness contrasted to my present despair came across me, I gave relief to the oppression of my heart that I felt by words, and groans, and heartrending sighs. But nature became wearied, and this more violent grief gave place to a passionate but mute flood of tears: my whole soul seemed to dissolve in them. I did not wring my hands, or tear my hair, or utter wild exclamations, but as Boccaccio describes the intense and quiet grief of Sigismunda over the heart of Guiscardo, I sat with my hands folded, silently letting fall a perpetual stream from my eyes. Such was the depth of my emotion that I had no feeling of what caused my distress, my thoughts even wandered to many indifferent objects. But still, neither moving limb or feature, my tears fell until, as if the fountains were exhausted, they gradually subsided, and I awoke to life as from a dream.

When I ceased to weep, reason and memory returned upon me, and I began to reflect with greater calmness on what had happened, and how it became me to act. A few hours only had passed, but a mighty revolution had taken place with regard to me—the natural work of years had been transacted since the morning. My father was as dead to me, and I felt for a moment as if he with white hairs were laid in his coffin and I, youth vanished in approaching age, were weeping at his timely dissolution. But it was not so, I was yet young—oh! far too young—nor was he dead to others; but I, most miserable, must never see or speak to him again. I must fly from him with more earnestness than from my greatest enemy. In solitude or in cities I must never more behold him. That consideration made me breathless with anguish and, impressing itself on my imagination, I was unable for a time to follow up any train of ideas.

Ever after this, I thought, I would live in the most dreary seclusion. I would retire to the Continent and become a nun; not for religion's sake, for I was not a Catholic, but that I might be forever shut out from the world. I should there find solitude where I might weep, and the voices of life might never reach me.

But my father—my beloved and most wretched father? Would he die? Would he never overcome the fierce passion that now held pitiless dominion over him? Might he not, many, many years hence, when age had quenched the burning sensations that he now experienced—might he not then be again a father to me? This reflection unwrinkled my brow, and I could feel (and I wept to feel it) a half melancholy smile draw from my lips their expression of suffering. I dared indulge better hopes for my future life. Years must pass but they would speed lightly away winged by hope, or if they passed heavily, still they would pass and I had not lost my father forever. Let him spend another sixteen years of desolate wandering: let him once more utter his wild complaints to the vast woods and the tremendous cataracts of another climate; let him again undergo fearful danger and soul-quelling hardships; let the hot sun of the south again burn his passion-worn cheeks and the cold night rain fall on him and chill his blood.

To this life, miserable father, I devote you! Go! Be your days passed with savages, and your nights under the cope of heaven! Be your limbs worn and your heart chilled, and all youth be dead within you! Let your hairs be as snow, your walk trembling, and your voice have lost its mellow tones! Let the liquid luster of your eyes be quenched; and then return to me, return to your Matilda, your child, who may then be clasped in your loved arms, while your heart beats with sinless emotion. Go, Devoted One, and return thus! This is my curse, a daughter's curse: Go, and return pure to your child, who will never love any but you.

These were my thoughts, and with trembling hands I prepared to begin a letter to my unhappy parent. I had now spent many hours in tears and mournful meditation; it was past twelve o'clock. All was at peace in the house, and the gentle air that stole in at my window did not rustle the leaves of the twining plants that shadowed it. I felt the entire tranquillity of the hour when my own breath and involuntary sobs were all the sounds that struck upon the air. Suddenly I heard a gentle step ascending the stairs; I paused breathless, and, as it approached, glided into an obscure corner of the room. The steps paused at my door, but after a few moments they again receded, descended the stairs and I heard no more.

This slight incident gave rise in me to the most painful reflections; nor do I now dare express the emotions I felt. That he should be restless I understood; that he should wander as an unlaid ghost and find no quiet from the burning hell that consumed his heart. But why approach my chamber? Was not that sacred? I felt almost ready to faint while he had stood there, but I had not betrayed my wakefulness by the slightest motion, although I had heard my own heart beat with violent fear. He had withdrawn. Oh, never, never, may I see him again! Tomorrow night the same roof may not cover us; he or I must depart. The mutual link of our destinies is broken; we must be divided by seas—by land. The stars and the sun must not rise at the same period to us. He must not say, looking at the setting crescent of the moon, "Matilda now watches its fall." Now, all must be changed. Be it light with him when it is darkness with me! Let him feel the sun of summer while I am chilled by the snows of winter! Let there be the distance of the antipodes between us!

At length the east began to brighten, and the comfortable light of morning streamed into my room. I was weary with watching, and for some time I had combated with the heavy sleep that weighed down my eyelids. But now, no longer fearful,

I threw myself on my bed. I sought for repose although I did not hope for forgetfulness; I knew I should be pursued by dreams, but did not dread the frightful one that I really had. I thought that I had risen and went to seek my father to inform him of my determination to separate myself from him. I sought him in the house, in the park, and then in the fields and the woods, but I could not find him. At length I saw him at some distance, seated under a tree, and, when he perceived me, he waved his hand several times, beckoning me to approach. There was something unearthly in his mien that awed and chilled me, but I drew near.

When at a short distance from him, I saw that he was deadly pale, and clothed in flowing garments of white. Suddenly he started up and fled from me; I pursued him. We sped over the fields, and by the skirts of woods, and on the banks of rivers. He flew fast and I followed. We came at last, I thought, to the brow of a huge cliff that overhung the sea, troubled by the winds, dashed against its base, at a distance. I heard the roar of the waters. He held his course right on towards the brink and I became breathless with fear lest he should plunge down the dreadful precipice. I tried to augment my speed, but my knees failed beneath me, yet I had just reached him—just caught a part of his flowing robe—when he leapt down and I awoke with a violent scream.

I was trembling and my pillow was wet with my tears. For a few moments my heart beat hard, but the bright beams of the sun and the chirping of the birds quickly restored me to myself, and I rose with a languid spirit, yet wondering what events the day would bring forth.

Some time passed before I summoned courage to ring the bell for my servant, and when she came, I still dared not utter my father's name. I ordered her to bring my breakfast to my room, and was again left alone—yet still I could make no resolve, but only thought that I might write a note to my father to beg his permission to pay a visit to a relation who lived about thirty miles off, and who had before invited me to her house, but I had refused, for then I could not quit my suffering father. When the servant came back she gave me a letter.

"From whom is this letter?" I asked trembling.

"Your father left it, madam, with his servant, to be given to you when you should rise."

"My father left it! Where is he? Is he not here?"

"No, he quitted the house before four this morning."

"Good God! He is gone! But tell how this was; speak quick!"

Her relation was short. He had gone in the carriage to the nearest town where he took a post chaise and horses with orders for the London road. He dismissed his servants there, only telling them that he had a sudden call of business, and that they were to obey me as their mistress until his return.

CHAPTER SEVEN

With a beating heart, and fearful, I knew not why, I dismissed the servant and, locking my door, sat down to read my father's letter. These are the words that it contained.

> My dear Child:
>
> I have betrayed your confidence; I have endeavored to pollute your mind, and have made your innocent heart acquainted with the looks and language of unlawful and monstrous passion. I must expiate these crimes, and must endeavor in some degree to proportionate my punishment to my guilt. You are, I doubt not, prepared for what I am about to announce; we must separate and be divided forever.
>
> I deprive you of your parent and only friend. You are cast out shelterless on the world: your hopes are blasted; the peace and security of your pure mind destroyed; memory will bring to you frightful images of guilt, and the anguish of innocent love betrayed. Yet I, who draw down all this misery upon you, I, who cast you forth and remorselessly have set the seal of distrust and agony on the heart and brow of my own child, who with devilish levity have endeavored to steal away her loveliness to place in its stead the foul deformity of sin, I, in the overflowing anguish of my heart, supplicate you to forgive me.
>
> I do not ask your pity; you must and do abhor me— but pardon me, Matilda, and let not your thoughts follow me in my banishment with unrelenting anger. I must nevermore behold you, nevermore hear your voice; but the soft whisperings of your forgiveness will reach me and cool the burning of my disordered brain and

heart; I am sure I should feel it even in my grave. And I dare enforce this request by relating how miserably I was betrayed into this net of fiery anguish, and all my struggles to release myself. Indeed, if your soul were less pure and bright, I would not attempt to exculpate myself to you; I should fear that if I led you to regard me with less abhorrence you might hate vice less—but, in addressing you, I feel as if I appealed to an angelic judge. I cannot depart without your forgiveness and I must endeavor to gain it, or I must despair. I conjure you therefore to listen to my words, and if, with the good, guilt may be in any degree extenuated by sharp agony, and remorse that rends the brain as madness, perhaps you may think, though I dare not, that I have some claim to your compassion.

I entreat you to call to your remembrance our first happy life on the shores of Loch Lomond. I had arrived from a weary wandering of sixteen years, during which, although I had gone through many dangers and misfortunes, my affections had been an entire blank. If I grieved, it was for your mother, if I loved, it was your image—these sole emotions filled my heart in quietness. The human creatures around me excited in me no sympathy, and I thought that the mighty change that the death of your mother had wrought within me had rendered me callous to any future impression. I saw the lovely and I did not love, I imagined therefore that all warmth was extinguished in my heart except that which led me ever to dwell on your then infantine image.

It is a strange link in my fate that, without having seen you, I should passionately love you. During my wanderings, I never slept without first calling down gentle dreams on your head. If I saw a lovely woman, I thought, does my Matilda resemble her? All delightful things, sublime scenery, soft breezes, exquisite music seemed to me associated with you, and only through you to be pleasant to me.

At length I saw you. You appeared as the deity of a lovely region, the ministering Angel of a Paradise to which, of all humankind, you admitted only me. I dared hardly consider you as my daughter—your beauty, artlessness and untaught wisdom seemed to belong to a higher order of beings; your voice breathed forth only words of love. If there was any of the Earthly in you, it was only what you derived from the beauty of the world. You seemed to have gained a grace from the mountain breezes—the waterfalls and the lake—and this was all of Earthly, except your affections, that you had; there was no dross, no bad feeling in the composition. You yet have not seen even enough of the world to know the stupendous difference that exists between the women we meet in daily life and the nymph of the woods such as you were, in whose eyes alone humankind may study for centuries and grow wider and purer. Those divine lights which shone on me as did those of Beatrice upon Dante, and well might I say with him, yet with what different feelings

E quasi mi perdei gli occhi chini
and nearly lost myself with lowered eyes

Can you wonder, Matilda, that I dwelt on your looks, your words, your motions, and drank in unmixed delight?

But I am afraid that I wander from my purpose. I must be more brief, for night draws on apace, and all my hours in this house are counted. Well, we removed to London, and still I felt only the peace of sinless passion. You were ever with me, and I desired no more than to gaze on your countenance, and to know that I was all the world to you; I was lapped in a fool's paradise of enjoyment and security. Was my love blamable? If it was, I was ignorant of it; I desired only that which

I possessed, and if I enjoyed from your looks, and words, and most innocent caresses a rapture usually excluded from the feelings of parent towards child, yet no uneasiness, no wish, no casual idea awoke me to a sense of guilt. I loved you as a human father might be supposed to love a daughter born to him by a heavenly mother; as Anchises might have regarded the child of Venus (if the sex had been changed)—love mingled with respect and adoration. Perhaps also my passion was lulled to content by the deep and exclusive affection you felt for me.

But when I saw you become the object of another's love, when I imagined that you might be loved otherwise than as a sacred type and image of loveliness and excellence, or that you might love another with a more ardent affection than that which you bore for me, then the fiend awoke within me. I dismissed your lover; and from that moment I have known no peace.

I have sought in vain for sleep and rest; my lids refused to close, and my blood was forever in a tumult. I awoke to a new life as one who dies in hope might wake in Hell. I will not sully your imagination by recounting my combats, my self-anger and my despair. Let a veil be drawn over the unimaginable sensations of a guilty father; the secrets of so agonized a heart may not be made vulgar. All was uproar, crime, remorse and hate, yet still the tenderest love; and what first awoke me to the firm resolve of conquering my passion, and of restoring her father to my child, was the sight of your bitter and sympathizing sorrows. It was this that led me here. I thought that, if I could again awaken in my heart the grief I had felt at the loss of your mother, and the many associations with her memory which had been laid to sleep for seventeen years, that all love for her child would become extinct.

In a fit of heroism I determined to go alone; to

quit you, the life of my life, and not to see you again until I might guiltlessly. But it would not do; I rated my fortitude too high, or my love too low. I should certainly have died if you had not hastened to me. Would that I had been indeed extinguished!

And now, Matilda, I must make you my last confession. I have been miserably mistaken in imagining that I could conquer my love for you; I never can. The sight of this house, these fields and woods which my first love inhabited, seems to have increased it. In my madness, I dared to say to myself: Diana died to give her birth; her mother's spirit was transferred to her frame, and she ought to be as Diana to me. With every effort to cast it off, this love clings closer, this guilty love more unnatural than hate, that withers your hopes and destroys me forever.

> Better have loved despair, and safer kissed her.

No time or space can tear from my soul that which makes a part of it. Since my arrival here I have not for a moment ceased to feel the hell of passion which has been implanted in me to burn until all be cold, and stiff, and dead. Yet I will not die; alas! How dare I go where I may meet Diana, when I have disobeyed her last request; her last words said in a faint voice when all feeling but love, which survives all things else, was already dead—she then bade me make her child happy. That thought alone gives a double sting to death.

I will wander away from you, away from all life—in the solitude I shall seek, I alone shall breathe of human-kind. I must endure life; and, as it is my duty, so I shall until the grave, dreaded yet desired, receive me free from pain, for while I feel, it will be pain that must make up the whole sum of my sensations. Is not this a fearful curse that I labor under? Do I not look forward to a miserable future?

My child, if, after this life, I am permitted to see you again, if pain can purify the heart, mine will be pure. If remorse may expiate guilt, I shall be guiltless.

I have been at the door of your chamber. Everything is silent. You sleep. Do you indeed sleep, Matilda? Spirits of Good, behold the tears of my earnest prayer! Bless my child! Protect her from the selfish among her fellow creatures. Protect her from the agonies of passion, and the despair of disappointment! Peace, Hope and Love be your guardians, oh, you soul of my soul: you in whom I breathe!

I dare not read my letter over, for I have no time to write another—and yet I fear that some expression in it might displease me. Since I last saw you, I have been constantly employed in writing letters, and have several more to write; for I do not intend that anyone shall hear of me after I depart. I need not conjure you to look upon me as one of whom all links that once existed between us are broken. Your own delicacy will not allow you, I am convinced, to attempt to trace me. It is far better for your peace that you should be ignorant of my destination. You will not follow me, for when I banish myself would you nourish guilt by obtruding yourself upon me? You will not do this, I know you will not.

You must forget me and all the evil that I have taught you. Cast off the only gift that I have bestowed upon you, your grief, and rise from under my blighting influence as no flower so sweet ever did rise from beneath so much evil.

You will never hear from me again. Receive these then as the last words of mine that will ever reach you; and, although I have forfeited your filial love, yet regard them, I conjure you as a father's command. Resolutely shake off the wretchedness that this first misfortune in early life must occasion you. Bear boldly up against the storm.Continue wise and mild, but believe it is—and indeed it is—your duty to be happy. You are very young; let not this check for more than a moment retard your glorious course; hold on, beloved one. The sun of youth is not set for you; it will restore vigor and life to you. Do not resist with obstinate grief its beneficent influence, oh, my child! Bless me with the hope that I have not utterly destroyed you.

Farewell, Matilda. I go with the belief that I have your pardon. Your gentle nature would not permit you to hate your greatest enemy and, though I be he, although I have rent happiness from your grasp, though I have passed over your young love and hopes as the angel of destruction—finding beauty and joy, and leaving blight and despair—yet you will forgive me, and with eyes overflowing with tears, I thank you. My beloved one, I accept your pardon with a gratitude that will never die, and that will, indeed it will, outlive guilt and remorse.

Farewell forever!

The moment I finished this letter I ordered the carriage and prepared to follow my father. The words of his letter by which he had dissuaded me from this step were those that determined me. Why did he write them? He must know that, if I believed that his intention was merely to absent himself from me—that instead of opposing him, it would be that which I should myself require. Or if he thought that any lurking feeling—yet he could not think that—should lead me to him, would he endeavor to overthrow the only hope he could have of ever seeing me again?

A lover—there was madness in the thought, yet he was my lover—would not act thus. No, he had determined to die, and he wished to spare me the misery of knowing it. The few ineffectual words he had said concerning his duty were to me a further proof—and the more I studied the letter the more did I perceive a thousand slight expressions that could only indicate a knowledge that life was now over for him. He was about to die! My blood froze at the thought: a sickening feeling of horror came over me that allowed not of tears. As I waited for the carriage, I walked up and down with a quick pace; then, kneeling and passionately clasping my hands I tried to pray, but my voice was choked by convulsive sobs. Oh, the sun shone, the air was balmy—he must yet live—for if he were dead all would surely be black as night to me!

The motion of the carriage, knowing that it carried me towards him and that I might perhaps find him alive, somewhat revived my courage; yet I had a dreadful ride. Hope only supported me, the hope that I should not be too late. I did not weep, but I wiped the perspiration from my brow, and tried to still my brain and heart beating almost to madness. I must not be mad when I see him; or perhaps it were as well that I should be, my distraction might calm his, and recall him to the endurance of life. Yet, until I find him, I must force reason to keep its seat, and I pressed my forehead hard with my hands.

—Oh do not leave me; or I shall forget what I am about. Instead of driving on as we ought with the speed of lightning, they will attend to me, and we shall be too late.

Oh God help me! Let him be alive! It is all dark; in my abject misery I demand no more—no hope, no good; only passion, and guilt, and horror—but alive! My sensations choked me—no tears fell, yet I sobbed, and breathed short and hard; one only thought possessed me, and I could only utter one word that half screaming was perpetually on my lips: Alive! Alive!—

I had taken the steward with me for he, much better than I, could make the requisite enquiries. The poor old man could not restrain his tears as he saw my deep distress and knew the cause. He sometimes uttered a few broken words of consolation. In moments such as these, the mistress and servant become in manner equals, and when I saw his old dim eyes wet with sympathizing tears, his gray hair thinly scattered on an age-wrinkled brow, I thought. Oh, if my father were as he is—

decrepit and hoary—then I should be spared this pain.

When I had arrived at the nearest town I took post horses and followed the road my father had taken. At every inn where we changed horses we heard of him, and I was possessed by alternates, hope and fear. At length I found that he had altered his route; at first he had followed the London road, but now he changed it, and upon enquiry I found that the one which he now pursued led towards the sea. My dream recurred to my thoughts; I was not usually superstitious, but, in wretchedness, everyone is so. The sea was fifty miles off, yet it was toward it that he fled. The idea was terrible to my half-crazed imagination, and almost overturned the little self-possession that still remained to me.

I journeyed all day; every moment my misery increased and the fever of my blood became intolerable. The summer sun shone in an unclouded sky; the air was close but all was cool to me except my own scorching skin. Toward evening, dark thunder clouds arose above the horizon and I heard its distant roll. After sunset they darkened the whole sky, and it began to rain. The lightning lighted up the whole country and the thunder drowned the noise of our carriage. At the next inn my father had not taken horses; he had left a box there saying he would return, and had walked over the fields to the town of _____, a seacoast town eight miles off.

For a moment I was almost paralyzed by fear; but my energy returned and I demanded a guide to accompany me in following his steps. The night was tempestuous, but my bribe was high and I easily procured a countryman. We passed through many lanes and over fields and wild downs; the rain poured down in torrents, and the loud thunder broke in terrible crashes over our heads. What a night it was! And I passed on with quick steps among the high, dank grass amid the rain and tempest. My dream was forever in my thoughts, and with a kind of half insanity that often possesses the mind in despair, I said aloud: "Courage! We are not near the sea; we are yet several miles from the ocean." Yet it was towards the sea that our direction lay and that heightened the confusion of my ideas.

Once, overcome by fatigue, I sank on the wet earth. About two hundred yards distant, alone in a large meadow, stood a magnificent oak; the lightning showed its myriad boughs torn by the storm. A strange idea seized me; a person must have felt all the agonies of doubt concerning the life and death of one who is the whole world to them before they can enter into my feelings—for in that state, the mind working unrestrained by the will makes strange and fanciful combinations with outward circumstances and weaves the chances and changes of nature into an immediate connection with the event they dread. It was with this feeling that I turned to the old steward, who stood pale and trembling beside me. "Mark, Gaspar, if the next flash of lightning rend not that oak my father will be alive."

I had scarcely uttered these words than a flash instantly followed by a tremendous peal of thunder descended on it; and when my eyes recovered their sight after the dazzling light, the oak no longer stood in the meadow. The old man uttered a wild exclamation of horror when he saw so sudden an interpretation given to my prophecy. I started up, my strength returned with my terror; I cried, "Oh, God! Is this your decree? Yet perhaps I shall not be too late."

Although still several miles distant we continued to approach the seas. We came at last to the road that led to the town of ____ and, at an inn there, we heard that my father had passed by somewhat before sunset. He had observed the approaching storm and had hired a horse for the next town, which was situated a mile from the sea that he might arrive there before it should commence; this town was five miles off. We hired a chaise here, and with four horses drove with speed through the storm. My garments were wet and clung around me, and my hair hung in straight locks on my neck when not blown aside by the wind. I shivered, yet my pulse was high with fever. Great God! What agony I endured. I shed no tears but my eyes wild and inflamed were starting from my head; I could hardly support the weight that pressed upon my brain.

We arrived at the town of ____ in a little more than half an hour.

When my father had arrived, the storm had already begun, but he had refused to stop, and, leaving his horse there, he walked on—towards the sea. Alas! it was double cruelty in him to have chosen the sea for his fatal resolve; it was adding madness to my despair.

The poor old servant who was with me tried to persuade me to remain here and to let him go alone. I shook my head silently and sadly; sick almost to death I leaned upon his arm, and as there was no road for a chaise, dragged my weary steps across the desolate downs to meet my fate, now too certain for the agony of doubt. Almost fainting, I slowly approached the fatal waters; when we had quitted the town, we heard their roaring. I whispered to myself in a muttering voice: "The sound is the same as that which I heard in my dream. It is the knell of my father which I hear."

The rain had ceased; there was no more thunder and lightning; the wind had paused. My heart no longer beat wildly; I did not feel any fever: but I was chilled; my knees sank under me—I almost slept as I walked with excess of weariness; every limb trembled. I was silent: all was silent except the roaring of the sea which became louder and more dreadful. Yet we advanced slowly: sometimes I thought that we should never arrive, that the sound of waves would still allure us, and that we should walk on forever and ever—field succeeding field, never would our weary journey cease, nor night nor day; but still we should hear the dashing of the sea, and to all this there would be no end. Wild beyond the imagination of the happy are the thoughts bred by misery and despair.

At length we reached the overhanging beach; a cottage stood beside the path. We knocked at the door and it was opened: the bed within instantly caught my eye; something stiff and straight lay on it, covered by a sheet; the cottagers looked aghast. The first words they uttered confirmed what I before knew. I did not feel shocked or overcome: I believe that I asked one or two questions and listened to the answers. I hardly know, but in a few moments I sank lifeless to the ground; and so would that then all had been at an end!

CHAPTER EIGHT

I was carried to the next town—fever succeeded to convulsions and faintings, and for some weeks my unhappy spirit hovered on the very verge of death. But life was yet strong within me; I recovered—nor did it a little aid my returning health that my recollections were at first vague, and that I was too weak to feel any violent emotion. I often said to myself, my father is dead. He loved me with a guilty passion, and, stung by remorse and despair, he killed himself. Why is it that I feel no horror? Are these circumstances not dreadful? Is it not enough that I shall never more meet the eyes of my beloved father; never more hear his voice; no caress, no look? All cold, and stiff, and dead! Alas! I am quite callous. The night I was out in was fearful, and the cold rain that fell about my heart has acted like the waters of the cavern of Antiparos and has changed it to stone. I do not weep or sigh; but I must reason with myself, and force myself to feel sorrow and despair. This is not resignation that I feel, for I am dead to all regret.

I communed in this manner with myself, but I was silent to all around me. I hardly replied to the slightest question, and was uneasy when I saw a human creature near me. I was surrounded by my female relations, but they were all of them nearly strangers to me. I did not listen to their consolations; and so little did they work their designed effect that they seemed to me to be spoken in an unknown tongue. I found if sorrow was dead within me, so was love and desire of sympathy. Yet sorrow only slept to revive more fierce, but love never woke again—its ghost, ever hovering over my father's grave, alone survived—since his death, all the world was to me a blank, except where woe had stamped its burning words telling me to smile no more—the living were not fit companions for me, and I was ever meditating by what means

I might shake them all off, and never be heard again.

My convalescence rapidly advanced, yet this was the thought that haunted me, and I was forever forming plans how I might hereafter contrive to escape the tortures that were prepared for me when I should mix in society, and to find that solitude which alone could suit one whom an untold grief separated from her fellow creatures. Who can be more solitary even in a crowd than one whose history and the never ending feelings and remembrances arising from it is known to no living soul?

There was too deep a horror in my tale for confidence; I was on Earth the sole depository of my secret. I might tell it to the winds and to the desert heaths but I must never among my fellow creatures, either by word or look give allowance to the smallest conjecture of the dread reality: I must shrink before the eye of man lest he should read my father's guilt in my glazed eyes. I must be silent lest my faltering voice should betray unimagined horrors. Over the deep grave of my secret I must heap an impenetrable heap of false smiles and words—cunning frauds, treacherous laughter, and a mixture of all light deceits would form a mist to blind others and be as the poisonous simoon to me. I, the offspring of love, the child of the woods, the nursling of Nature's bright self was to submit to this? I dared not.

How must I escape? I was rich and young, and had a guardian appointed for me; and all about me would act as if I were one of their great society, while I must keep the secret that I really was cut off from them forever. If I fled, I should be pursued; in life there was no escape for me. Why, then I must die. I shuddered; I dared not die even though the cold grave held all I loved— although I might say with Job:

> Where is now my hope? For my hope who shall see it?
> They shall go down together to the bars of the pit,
> when our rest together is in the dust—

Yes, my hope was corruption and dust and all to which death brings us. Or afterlife—no, no, I will not persuade myself to die, I may not, dare not. And then I wept; yes, warm tears once more struggled into my eyes, soothing yet bitter; and after I had wept much and called with unavailing anguish, with outstretched arms, for my cruel father, after my weak frame was exhausted by all variety of plaint, I sank once more into reverie, and once more reflected on how I might find that which I most desired—dear to me if anything were dear, a death-like solitude.

I dared not die, but I might feign death, and thus escape from my comforters. They will believe me united to my father, and so indeed I shall be. For alone, when no voice can disturb my dream, and no cold eye meet mine to check its fire, then I may commune with his spirit—on a lone heath, at noon or at midnight, still I should be near him. His last injunction to me was that I should be happy; perhaps he did not mean the shadowy happiness that I promised myself, yet it was that alone which I could taste. He did not conceive that ever again I could make one of the smiling hunters that go coursing after bubbles that break to nothing when caught, and then after a new one with brighter colors. My hope also had proved a bubble, but it had been so lovely, so adorned that I saw none that could attract me after it; besides, I was wearied with the pursuit, nearly dead with weariness.

I would feign to die; my contented heirs would seize upon my wealth, and I should purchase freedom. But then my plan must be laid with art; I would not be left destitute, I must secure some money. Alas! To what loathsome shifts must I be driven? Yet a whole life of falsehood was otherwise my portion—and when remorse at being the contriver of any cheat made me shrink from my design, I was irresistibly led back and confirmed in it by the visit of some aunt or cousin, who would tell me that death was the end of all men. And then say that my father had surely lost his wits ever since my mother's death; that he was mad and that I was fortunate, for in one of his fits he might have killed me instead of destroying his own crazed being. And all this, to be sure, was delicately put; not in broad words for my feelings might be hurt but with downcast eyes, and sympathizing smiles or whimpers; and I listened with quiet countenance while every nerve trembled; I that dared not utter aye or no to all this blasphemy. Oh, this was a delicious life quite void of guile! I ,with my dove's look and fox's heart, for indeed I felt only the degradation of falsehood, and not any sacred sentiment of conscious innocence that might redeem it. I, who had before clothed myself in the bright garb of sincerity, must now borrow one of diverse colors; it might sit awkwardly at first, but use would enable me to place it in elegant folds, to lie with grace. Aye, I might dye my soul with falsehood until I had quite hid its native color.

Oh, beloved father! Accept the pure heart of your unhappy daughter; permit me to join you unspotted as I was, or you will not recognize my altered semblance. As grief might change Constance so would deceit change me until in heaven you would say, "This is not my child." My father, to be happy, both now and when again we meet, I must fly from all this life which is mockery to one like me. In solitude only shall I be myself; in solitude I shall be yours.

Alas! I even now look back with disgust at my artifices and contrivances by which, after many painful struggles, I effected my retreat. I might enter into a long detail of the means I used, first to secure myself a slight maintenance for the remainder of my life, and afterwards, to ensure the conviction of my death. I might, but I will not. I even now blush to the falsehoods I uttered; my heart sickens. I will leave this complication, of what I hope I may in a manner call innocent deceit, to be imagined by the reader. The remembrance haunts me like a crime—I know that, if I were to endeavor to relate it, my tale would at length remain unfinished.

I was led to London, and had to endure for some weeks cold looks, cold words and colder consolations—but I escaped. They tried to bind me with fetters that they thought silken, yet which weighed on me like iron, although I broke them more easily than a girth formed of a single straw, and fled to London.

The few weeks that I spent in London were the most miserable of my life. A great city is a frightful habitation to one sorrowing. The sunset and the gentle moon, the blessed motion of the leaves and the murmuring of waters are all sweet physicians to a distempered mind. The soul is expanded and drinks in quiet, a lulling medicine—to me it was as the sight of the lovely water snakes to the bewitched mariner—in loving and blessing Nature I, unawares, called down a blessing on my own soul. But in a city all is closed shut like a prison, a wiry prison from which you can peep at the sky only. I cannot describe to you what was the frantic nature of my sensations while I resided there; I was often on the verge of madness. Nay, when I look back on many of my wild thoughts—thoughts with which actions sometimes endeavored to keep pace—when I tossed my hands high, calling down the cope of heaven to fall on me and bury me, when I tore my hair and throwing it to the winds cried, "You are free, go seek my father!" And then, like the unfortunate Constance, catching them again and tying them up, that no one might find him if I might not. How, on my knees, I have fancied myself close to my father's grave and struck the ground in anger that it should cover him from me. Oft when I have listened with gasping attention for the sound of the ocean mingled with my father's groans—and then wept until my strength was gone and I was calm and faint—when I have recollected all this, I have asked myself if this were not madness. While in London, these and many other dreadful thoughts too harrowing for words were my portion. I lost all this suffering when I was free; when I saw the wild heath around me, and the evening star in the west, then I could weep, gently weep, and be at peace.

Do not mistake me; I never was really mad. I was always conscious of my state when my wild thoughts seemed to drive me to insanity, and never betrayed them to aught but silence and solitude. The people around me saw nothing of all this. They only saw a poor young woman broken in spirit, who spoke in a low and gentle voice, and from underneath whose downcast lids tears would sometimes steal which she strove to hide. One who loved to be alone, and shrunk from observation, who never smiled—Oh, no! I never smiled—and that was all.

Well, I escaped. I left my guardian's house and I was never heard of again. It was believed from the letters that I left, and other circumstances that I planned, that I had destroyed myself. I was sought after therefore with less care than would otherwise have been the case. Soon all trace and memory of me was lost.

I left London in a small vessel bound for a port in the north of England. And now, having succeeded in my attempt, and being quite alone, peace returned to me. The sea was calm and the vessel moved gently onwards. I sat upon deck under the open canopy of heaven and thought I was an altered creature. Not the wild, raving and most miserable Matilda, but a youthful hermit dedicated to seclusion and whose bosom she must strive to keep free from all tumult and unholy despair. The fanciful nun-like dress that I had adopted; the knowledge that my very existence was a secret known only to myself; the solitude to which I was forever hereafter destined, nursed gentle thoughts in my wounded heart. The breeze that played in my hair revived me, and I watched with quiet eyes the sunbeams that glittered on the waves, and the birds that chased each other over the waters, just brushing them with their plumes. I slept too, undisturbed by dreams, and awoke refreshed to again enjoy my tranquil freedom.

In four days, we arrived at the harbor to which we were bound. I would not remain on the sea coast, but proceeded immediately inland. I had already planned the situation where I would live. It should be a solitary house on a wide plain near no other habitation, where I could behold the whole horizon, and wander far without molestation from the sight of my fellow creatures. I was not misanthropic, but I felt that the gentle current of my feelings depended upon my being alone. I fixed myself on a wide solitude, on a dreary heath bestrewn with stones, among which short grass grew, and here and there a few rushes beside a little pool. Not far from my cottage was a small cluster of pines, the only trees to be seen for many miles. I had a path cut through the furze from my door to this little wood, from whose topmost branches the birds saluted the rising sun and awoke me to my daily meditation. My view was bounded only by the horizon, except on one side where a distant wood made a black spot on the heath, that everywhere else stretched out its faint hues as far as the eye could reach—wide and very desolate. Here I could mark the network of the clouds as they wove themselves into thick masses, I could watch the slow rise of the heavy thunder clouds and could see the rack as it was driven across the heavens—or under the pine trees I could enjoy the stillness of the azure sky.

My life was very peaceful. I had one woman servant who spent the greater part of the day at a village two miles off. My amusements were simple and very innocent; I fed the birds who built on the pines or among the ivy that covered the wall of my little garden. And they soon knew me; the bolder ones pecked the crumbs from my hands and perched on my fingers to sing their thankfulness. When I had lived here some time, other animals visited me—a fox came every day for a portion of food appropriated for him and would suffer me to pat his head. I had, besides, many books and a harp with which, when despairing, I could soothe my spirits, and raise myself to sympathy and love.

Love! What had I to love? Oh, many things—there was the moonshine, and the bright stars; the breezes and the refreshing rains; there was the whole Earth and the sky that covers it— all lovely forms that visited my imagination, all memories of heroism and virtue. Yet this was very unlike my early life, although as then, I was confined to Nature and books. Then, I bounded across the fields; my spirit often seemed to ride upon the winds, and to mingle in joyful sympathy with the ambient air. Then, if I wandered slowly, I cheered myself with a sweet song or sweeter daydreams. I felt a holy rapture spring from all I saw. I drank in joy with my life; my steps were light; my eyes, clear from love that animated them, sought the heavens, and, with my long hair loosened to the winds, I gave my body and my mind to sympathy and delight.

But now my walk was slow—My eyes were seldom raised and often filled with tears. No song, no smiles, no careless motion that might bespeak a mind intent on what surrounded it. I was gathered up into myself—a selfish solitary creature ever pondering on my regrets and faded hopes.

Mine was an idle, useless life; it was so—but say not to the lily laid prostrate by the storm—Arise, and bloom as before. My heart was bleeding from its death's wound; I could live no otherwise. Often, amid apparent calm, I was visited by despair and melancholy; gloom that nought could dissipate or overcome; a hatred of life; a carelessness of beauty—all these would by fits hold me nearly annihilated by their powers. Never for one moment, when most placid, did I cease to pray for death. I could be found in no state of mind which I would not willingly have exchanged for nothingness. And morning and evening my tearful eyes raised to heaven, my hands clasped tight in the energy of prayer, I have repeated with the poet—

> Before I see another day
> Oh, let this body die away!

Let me not be reproached then with inutility. I believed that, by suicide, I should violate a divine law of nature, and I thought that I sufficiently fulfilled my part in submitting to the hard task of enduring the crawling hours and minutes—in bearing the load of time that weighed miserably upon me, and that, in abstaining from what I in my calm moments considered a crime, I deserved the reward of virtue. There were periods, dreadful ones, during which I despaired—and doubted the existence of all duty and the reality of crime—but I shudder, and turn from the remembrance.

CHAPTER NINE

Thus I passed two years. Day after day—so many hundreds wore on; they brought no outward changes with them, but some few slowly operated on my mind as I glided on towards death.

I began to study more; to sympathize more in the thoughts of others as expressed in books, to read history, and to lose my individuality among the crowd that had existed before me. Thus, perhaps as the sensation of immediate suffering wore off, I became more human. Solitude also lost to me some of its charms. I began again to wish for sympathy—not that I was ever tempted to seek the crowd, but I wished for one friend to love me. You will say perhaps that I gradually became fitted to return to society. I do not think so—for the sympathy that I desired must be so pure, so divested of influence from outward circumstances that, in the world, I could not fail of being balked by the gross materials that perpetually mingle even with its best feelings.

Believe me, I was then less fitted for any communion with my fellow creatures than before. When I left them, they had tormented me, but it was in the same way as pain and sickness may torment—something extraneous to the mind that galled it, and that I wished to cast aside. But now I should have desired sympathy; I should wish to knit my soul to some one of theirs, and should have prepared for myself plentiful drafts of disappointment and suffering, for I was tender as the sensitive plant—all nerve. I did not desire sympathy and aid in ambition or wisdom, but sweet and mutual affection, smiles to cheer me, and gentle words of comfort. I wished for one heart in which I could pour unrestrained my plaints, and, by the heavenly nature of the soil, blessed fruit might spring from such bad seed. Yet how could I find this? The love that is the soul of friendship is a soft spirit seldom found, except when two amiable creatures are knit from early youth, or when bound by mutual suffering and pursuits. It comes to some of the elect unsought and unaware; it descends as gentle dew on chosen spots which, however barren they were before, become under its benign influence fertile in all sweet plants—but when desired it flies. It scoffs at the prayers of its votaries; it will bestow, but not be sought.

I knew all this and did not go to seek sympathy, but, there on my solitary heath, under my lowly roof where all around was desert, it came to me as a sunbeam in winter, to adorn while it helps to dissolve the drifted snow. Alas, the sun shone on blighted fruit. I did not revive under its radiance, for I was too utterly undone to feel its kindly power. My father had been—and his memory was—the life of my life. I might feel gratitude to another but I never more could love or hope as I had done. It was all suffering; even my pleasures were endured, not enjoyed.

I was a solitary spot among mountains, shut in on all sides by steep black precipices, where no ray of heat could penetrate, and from which there was no outlet to sunnier fields. And thus it was that, although the spirit of friendship soothed me for a while, it could not restore me. It came as some gentle visitation; it went and I hardly felt the loss. The spirit of existence was dead within me. Be not surprised therefore that ,when it came, I welcomed not more gladly, or when it departed, I lamented not more bitterly the best gift of heaven—a friend.

The name of my friend was Woodville. I will briefly relate his history that you may judge how cold my heart must have been not to be warmed by his eloquent words and tender sympathy, and how he, also being most unhappy, we were well fitted to be a mutual consolation to each other—if I had not been hardened to stone by the Medusa head of Misery. The misfortunes of Woodville were not of the heart's core like mine; his was a natural grief, not to destroy but to purify the heart, and from which he might, when its shadow had passed from over him, shine forth brighter and happier than before.

Woodville was the son of a poor clergyman and had received

a classical education. He was one of those very few whom fortune favors from their birth, on whom she bestows all gifts of intellect and person with a profusion that knew no bounds, and whom under her peculiar protection, no imperfection, however slight, or disappointment, however transitory, has leave to touch. She seemed to have formed his mind of that excellence which no dross can tarnish, and his understanding was such that no error could pervert. His genius was transcendent, and when it rose as a bright star in the East all eyes were turned towards it in admiration.

He was a Poet. That name has so often been degraded that it will not convey the idea of all that he was. He was like a poet of old, whom the muses had crowned in his cradle, and on whose lips bees had fed. As he walked among other men, he seemed encompassed with a heavenly halo that divided him from, and lifted him above, them. It was his surpassing beauty, the dazzling fire of his eyes, and his words, which rich accents wrapped the listener in mute and ecstatic wonder, that made him transcend all others so that, before him, they appeared only formed to minister to his superior excellence.

He was glorious from his youth. Everyone loved him; no shadow of envy or hate, cast even from the meanest mind, ever fell upon him. He was, as one peculiar delight of the Gods, railed and fenced in by his own divinity, so that nought but love and admiration could approach him. His heart was simple like a child, unstained by arrogance or vanity. He mingled in society, unknowing of his superiority over his companions, not because he undervalued himself, but because he did not perceive the inferiority of others. He seemed incapable of conceiving of the full extent of the power that selfishness and vice possesses in the world. When I knew him, although he had suffered disappointment in his dearest hopes, he had not experienced any that arose from the meanness and self-love of humans. His station was too high to allow of his suffering through their hardheartedness—and too low for him to have experienced ingratitude and encroaching selfishness. It is one

77

of the blessings of a moderate fortune, that, by preventing the possessor from conferring pecuniary favors, it prevents him also from diving into the arcana of human weakness or malice. To bestow on your fellow human being is a god-like attribute: so indeed it is, and as such not one fit for mortality. The giver, like Adam and Prometheus, must pay the penalty of rising above his nature by being the martyr to his own excellence.

Woodville was free from all these evils, and, if slight examples did come across him, he did not notice them but passed on in his course, as an angel with winged feet might glide along the Earth, unimpeded by all those little obstacles over which we of Earthly origin stumble. He was a believer in the divinity of genius and always opposed a stern disbelief to the objections of those petty cavillers and minor critics who wish to reduce all to their own miserable level. "I will make a scientific simile," he would say, "in the manner, if you will, of Dr. Darwin—I consider the alleged errors of one of genius as the aberrations of the fixed stars. It is our distance from them and our imperfect means of communication that makes them appear to move; in truth, they always remain stationary, a glorious center, giving us a fine lesson of modesty, if we would thus receive it."

I have said that he was a poet—when he was twenty-three years of age he first published a poem, and it was hailed by the whole nation with enthusiasm and delight. His good star perpetually shone upon him; a reputation had never before been made so rapidly—it was universal. The multitude extolled the same poems that formed the wonder of the sage in his closet; there was not one dissenting voice.

It was at this time, in the height of his glory, that he became acquainted with Elinor. She was a young heiress of exquisite beauty, who lived under the care of her guardian. From the moment they were seen together, they appeared formed for each other. Elinor had not the genius of Woodville, but she was generous and noble, and exalted by her youth and the love that she everywhere excited, above the knowledge of aught but virtue and excellence. She was lovely; her manners were frank and simple; her deep blue eyes swam in a luster which could only be given by sensibility joined to wisdom.

They were formed for each other and they soon loved. Woodville for the first time felt the delight of love; and Elinor was enraptured in possessing the heart of one so beautiful and glorious among his fellow humans. Could anything but unmixed joy flow from such a union?

Woodville was a Poet—he was sought for by every society, and all eyes were turned on him alone when he appeared. But he was the son of a poor clergyman, and Elinor was a rich heiress. Her guardian was not displeased with their mutual affection— the merit of Woodville was too eminent to admit of cavil on account of his inferior wealth. But the dying will of her father did not allow her to marry before she was of age, and her fortune depended upon her obeying this injunction. She had just entered her twentieth year, and she and her lover were obliged to submit to this delay. But they were ever together and their happiness seemed that of Paradise. They studied together, formed plans of future occupations, and—drinking in love and joy from each other's eyes and words—they hardly repined at the delay to their entire union. Woodville forever rose in glory; and Elinor became more lovely and wise under the lessons of her accomplished lover.

In two months Elinor would be twenty-one: everything was prepared for their union. How shall I relate the catastrophe to so much joy? But the Earth would not be the Earth it is, covered with blight and sorrow, if one such pair as these angelic creatures had been suffered to exist for one another. Search through the world, and you will not find the perfect happiness which their marriage would have caused them to enjoy. There must have been a revolution in the order of things as established among us miserable Earthdwellers to have admitted of such consummate joy. The chain of necessity, ever bringing misery, must have been broken, and the malignant fate that presides over it would not permit this breach of her eternal laws. But why should I repine at this? Misery was my element, and nothing but what was miserable could approach me. If Woodville had been happy, I should never have known him. And can I, who for many years was fed by tears, and nourished under the dew of grief—can I pause to relate a tale of woe and death?

Woodville was obliged to make a journey into the country, and was detained from day to day in irksome absence from his lovely bride. He received a letter from her to say that she was slightly ill, but telling him to hasten to her—that, from his eyes, she would receive health, and that his company would be her surest medicine. He was detained three days longer and then he hastened to her. His heart, he knew not why, prognosticated misfortune; he had not heard from her again. He feared she might be worse and this fear made him impatient and restless for the moment of beholding her once more stand before him arrayed in health and beauty—for a sinister voice seemed always to whisper to him, "You will never more behold her as she was."

When he arrived at her habitation, all was silent in it. He made his way through several rooms; in one he saw a servant weeping bitterly. He was faint with fear and could hardly ask, "Is she dead?" and just listened to the dreadful answer, "Not yet." These astounding words came on him as of less fearful import than those which he had expected. To learn that she was still in being, and that he might still hope, was an alleviation to him. He remembered the words of her letter, and he indulged the wild idea that his kisses breathing warm love and life would infuse new spirit into her—and that, with him near, she could not die, that his presence was the talisman of her life.

He hastened to her sick room. She lay, her cheeks burning with fever, yet her eyes were closed and she was seemingly senseless. He wrapped her in his arms, he imprinted breathless kisses on he burning lips. He called to her in a voice of subdued anguish by the tenderest names: "Return Elinor; I am with you; your life, your love. Return; dearest one, you promised me this boon, that I should bring you health. Let your sweet spirit revive; you cannot die near me. What is death? To see you no more? To part with what is a part of myself, without whom I have no memory and no futurity? Elinor die! This is frenzy and the most miserable despair. You cannot die while I am near."

And again he kissed her eyes and lips, and hung over her inanimate form in agony, gazing on her countenance, still lovely although changed, watching every slight convulsion and varying color, which denoted life still lingering, although about to depart. Once, for a moment, she revived and recognized his voice. A smile, a last lovely smile, played upon her lips. He watched beside her for twelve hours, and then she died.

Chapter Ten

It was six months after this miserable conclusion to his long-nursed hopes that I first saw him. He had retired to a part of the country where he was not known, that he might peacefully indulge his grief. All the world, by the death of his beloved Elinor, was changed to him, and he could no longer remain in any spot where he had seen her, or where her image, mingled with the most rapturous hopes, had blightened all around with a light of joy which would now be transformed to a darkness blacker than midnight since she, the sun of his life, was set forever.

He lived for some time never looking on the light of heaven but shrouding his eyes in a perpetual darkness, far from all that could remind him of what he had been. But, as time softened his grief, like a true child of Nature he sought in the enjoyment of its beauties for a consolation in his unhappiness. He came to a part of the country where he was entirely unknown, and where in the deepest solitude he could converse only with his own heart. He found a relief to his impatient grief in the breezes of heaven and in the sound of waters and woods. He became fond of riding; this exercise distracted his mind and elevated his spirits; on a swift horse he could, for a moment, gain respite from the image that else forever followed him—Elinor on her death bed, her sweet features changed, and the soft spirit that animated her gradually waning into extinction.

For many months Woodville had in vain endeavored to cast off this terrible remembrance; it still hung on him until memory was too great a burden for his loaded soul, but when on horseback the spell that seemingly held him to this idea was snapped—then, if he thought of his lost bride, he pictured her radiant in beauty. He could hear her voice, and fancy her "a sylvan Hunter by his side," while his eyes brightened as he thought he gazed on her cherished form.

I had several times seen him ride across the heath, and felt angry that my solitude should be disturbed. It was so long since I had spoken to any but the local people, that I felt a disagreeable sensation at being gazed on by someone more sophisticated. I feared also that it might be someone who had seen me before. I might be recognized, my impostures discovered and I dragged back to a life of worse torture than I had before endured. These were dreadful fears and they even haunted my dreams.

I was one day seated on the verge of the clump of pines when Woodville rode past. As soon as I perceived him, I suddenly rose to escape from his observation by entering among the trees. My rising startled his horse; he reared and plunged, and the rider was at length thrown. The horse then galloped swiftly across the heath, and the stranger remained on the ground, stunned by his fall. He was not materially hurt—a little fresh water soon recovered him. I was struck by his exceeding beauty, and, as he spoke to thank me, the sweet but melancholy cadence of his voice brought tears into my eyes.

A short conversation passed between us, but the next day he again stopped at my cottage, and by degrees an intimacy grew between us. It was strange to him to see a female in extreme youth—I was not yet twenty—evidently belonging to the first classes of society and possessing every accomplishment an excellent education could bestow, living alone on a desolate heath—one on whose forehead the impress of grief was strongly marked, and whose words and motions betrayed that her thoughts did not follow them but were intent on far other ideas: bitter and overwhelming miseries. I was dressed also in a whimsical nun-like habit, which denoted that I did not retire to solitude from necessity, but that I might indulge in a luxury of grief, and fanciful seclusion.

He soon took great interest in me, and sometimes forgot his own grief to sit beside me and endeavor to cheer me. He could not fail to interest even one who had shut herself from the whole world, whose hope was death, and who lived only with the departed. His personal beauty, his conversation which glowed with imagination and sensibility, the poetry that seemed to hang upon his lips and to make the very air mute to listen to him—were charms that no one could resist. He was younger, less worn, more passionless than my father and in no degree reminded me of him. He suffered under immediate grief, yet its gentle influence, instead of calling feelings otherwise dormant into action, seemed only to veil that which otherwise would have been too dazzling for me. When we were together, I spoke little yet of my selfish mind—was sometimes borne away by the rapid course of his ideas. I would lift my eyes with momentary brilliancy, until memories that never died and seldom slept would recur, and a tear would dim them.

Woodville forever tried to lead me to the contemplation of what is beautiful and happy in the world. His own mind was constitutionally bent to a former belief in good rather than in evil, and this feeling, which must even exhilarate the hopeless, ever shone forth in his words. He would talk of the wonderful powers of human beings, of their present state and of their hopes—of what they had been and what they were. And when reason could no longer guide him, his imagination, as if inspired, shed light on the obscurity that veils the past and the future.

He loved to dwell on what might have been the state of the Earth before humans lived on it, and how they first arose and became the strange, complicated, but, as he said, the glorious creatures they now are. Covering the Earth with their creations and forming, by the power of their minds, another world more lovely than the visible frame of things—even all the world that we find in their writings. A beautiful creation, he would say, which may claim this superiority to its model—that good and evil is more easily separated: the good rewarded in the way they themselves desire; the evil punished as all things evil ought to be punished—not by pain, which is revolting to all philanthropy to consider, but by quiet obscurity, which simply deprives them of their harmful qualities. Why kill the serpent when you have extracted his fangs?

The poetry of his language and ideas, which my words ill convey, held me enchained to his discourses. It was a melancholy pleasure to me to listen to his inspired words, to catch for a moment the light of his eyes, to feel a transient sympathy—and then to awaken from the delusion, again to know that all this was nothing—a dream—a shadow; for that, there was no reality for me; my father had forever deserted me, leaving me only memories, which set an eternal barrier between me and my fellow creatures.

I was indeed fellow to none. He—Woodville—mourned the loss of his bride. Others wept the various forms of misery as they visited them—but infamy and guilt were mingled with my portion. Unlawful and detestable passion had poured its poison into my ears and changed all my blood, so that it was no longer the kindly stream that supports life, but a cold fountain of bitterness corrupted in its very source. It must be the excess of madness that could make me imagine that I could ever be anything but one alone—struck off from humanity, bearing no affinity to man or woman, a wretch on whom Nature had set its ban.

Sometimes Woodville talked to me of himself. He related his history brief in happiness and woe, and dwelt with passion on his and Elinor's mutual love.

"She was," he said, "the brightest vision that ever came upon the Earth. There was something in her frank countenance, in her voice, and in every motion of her graceful form that overpowered me, as if it were a celestial creature that deigned to mingle with me in intercourse more sweet than humanity had ever before enjoyed. Sorrow fled before her; and her smile seemed to possess an influence like light to irradiate all mental darkness. It was not like a human loveliness that these gentle smiles went and came; but as a sunbeam on a lake, now light and now obscure, flitting before as you strove to catch them, and fold them forever to your heart. I saw this smile fade forever. Alas! I could never have believed that it was indeed Elinor that died, if once, when I spoke she had not lifted her almost benighted eyes, and for one moment like nought beside on Earth, more lovely than a sunbeam, slighter, quicker than the waving plumage of a bird, dazzling as lightning and, like it, giving day to night—yet mild and faint, that smile came. It went, and then there was an end of all joy to me."

Thus his own sorrows, or the shapes copied from nature that dwelt in his mind with beauty greater than their own, occupied our talk—while I railed in my own griefs with cautious secrecy. If for a moment he showed curiosity, my eyes fell, my voice died away and my evident suffering made him quickly endeavor to banish the ideas he had awakened. Yet he forever mingled consolation in his talk, and tried to soften my despair by demonstrations of deep sympathy and compassion.

"We are both unhappy," he would say to me; "I have told you my melancholy tale, and we have wept together the loss of that lovely spirit that has so cruelly deserted me. But you hide your griefs. I do not ask you to disclose them, but tell me if I may not console you. It seems to me a wild adventure to find in this desert one like you quite solitary. You are young and lovely; your manners are refined and attractive—yet there is in your settled melancholy, a something, I know not what, in your expressive eyes that seems to separate you from your kind. You shudder; you pardon me, I entreat you, but I cannot help expressing, this once at least, the lively interest I feel in your destiny.

"You never smile, your voice is low, and you utter your words as if you were afraid of the slight sound they would produce. The expression of awful and intense sorrow never for a moment fades from your countenance. I have lost forever the loveliest companion that any man could ever have had, one who rather appears to have been a superior spirit, who by some strange accident wandered among us Earthly creatures, than as belonging to our kind. Yet I smile, and sometimes I speak almost forgetful of the change I have endured.

"But your sad mien never alters; your pulses beat and you breathe, yet you seem already to belong to another world. And sometimes, pray pardon my wild thoughts, when you touch my hand, I am surprised to find your warm hand, when all the fire of life seems extinct within you.

"When I look upon you, the tears you shed, the soft deprecating look with which you withstand enquiry, the deep sympathy your voice expresses when I speak of my lesser sorrows, add to my interest for you. You stand here shelterless. You have cast yourself from among us, and you wither on this wild plain, forlorn and helpless. Some dreadful calamity must have befallen you. Do not turn from me; I do not ask you to reveal it. I only entreat you to listen to me, and to become familiar with the voice of consolation and kindness. If pity and admiration and gentle affection can wean you from despair, let me attempt the task. I cannot see your look of deep grief without endeavoring to restore you to happier feelings. Unbend your brow; relax the stern melancholy of your regard. Permit a friend, a sincere, affectionate friend—I will be one—to convey some relief, some momentary pause to your sufferings.

"Do not think that I would intrude upon your confidences. I only ask your patience. Do not forever look sorrow and never speak it. Utter one word of bitter complaint, and I will reprove it with gentle exhortation and pour on you the balm of compassion. You must not shut me from all communion with you. Do not tell me why you grieve, but only say the words, 'I am unhappy,' and you will feel relieved as if, for some time excluded from all intercourse by some magic spell, you should suddenly enter again the pale of human sympathy. I entreat you to believe in my most sincere profession and to treat me as an old and tried friend. Promise me never to forget me, never causelessly to banish me, but try to love me as one who would devote all his energies to make you happy. Give me the name of friend. I will fulfill its duties, and if, for a moment, complaint and sorrow would shape themselves into words, let me be near to speak peace to your vexed soul."

I repeat his persuasions in faint terms and cannot give you at the same time the tone and gesture that animated them. Like a refreshing shower on an arid soil they revived me, and, although I still kept their cause secret, he led me to pour forth my bitter complaints and to clothe my woe in words of gall and fire. With all the energy of desperate grief I told him how I had fallen at one from bliss to misery, how that for me there was no joy, no hope—that death, however bitter, would be the welcome seal to all my pangs—death the skeleton was to be beautiful as love. I know not why but I found it sweet to utter these words to human ears. And though I derided all consolation, yet I was pleased to see it offered me with gentleness and kindness. I listened quietly, and, when he paused, I would again pour out my misery in expressions that showed how far too deep my wounds were for any cure.

But now also I began to reap the fruits of my perfect solitude. I had become unfit for any intercourse, even with Woodville the most gentle and sympathizing creature that existed. I had become captious and unreasonable—my temper was utterly spoiled. I called him my friend, but I viewed all he did with jealous eyes. If he did not visit me at the appointed hour I was angry—very angry—and told him that if indeed he did feel interest in me it was cold, and could not be fitted for me, a poor worn creature, whose deep unhappiness demanded much more than his worldly heart could give.

When, for a moment, I imagined that his manner was cold, I would fretfully say to him, "I was at peace before you came. Why have you disturbed me? You have given me new wants, and now you trifle with me as if my heart were as whole as yours, as if I were not in truth a shorn lamb thrust out on the bleak hillside, tortured by every blast. I wished for no friend, no sympathy. I avoided you, you know I did, but you forced yourself upon me and gave me those wants which, you see with triumph, give you power over me. Oh, the brave power of the bitter north wind which freezes the tears it has caused to shed! But I will not bear this. Go. The sun will rise and set as before you came, and I shall sit among the pines or wander on the heath weeping and complaining without wishing for you to listen. You are very cruel, very cruel, to treat me who bleed at every pore in this rough manner."

And then, when in answer to my peevish words, I saw his face bent with living pity on me, when I saw him

> Gli occhi drizzo ver me con quel sembiante
> Che madre fa sopra figlioul deliro
> > his eyes on me with the same look
> > that a mother gives to a bratty child

I wept and said, "Oh pardon me! You are good and kind, but I am not fit for life. Why am I obliged to live? To drag hour after hour, to see the trees wave their branches restlessly, to feel the air, and to suffer in all I feel, keenest agony. My frame is strong, but my soul sinks beneath this endurance of living anguish. Death is the goal that I would attain, but, alas! I do not even see the end of the course. Do you, my compassionate friend, tell me how to die peacefully and innocently, and I will bless you. All that I, poor wretch, can desire is a painless death."

But Woodville's words had magic in them, when, beginning with the sweetest pity, he would raise me by degrees out of myself and my sorrows until I wondered at my own selfishness. But he left me, and despair returned. The world of consolation was ever to begin anew.

I often desired his entire absence, for I found that I was grown out of the ways of life, and that, by long seclusion, although I could support my accustomed grief and drink the bitter daily draught with some degree of patience, yet I had become unfit for the slightest novelty of feeling. Expectation and hope and affection were all too much for me. I knew this, but at other times I was unreasonable, and laid the blame upon him, who was most blameless, and I peevishly thought that, if his gentle soul were more gentle, if his intense sympathy were more intense, he could drive the fiend from my soul and make me more human.

I am, I thought, a tragedy—a character that he comes to see act. Now and then, he gives me my cue that I may make a speech more to his purpose. Perhaps he is already planning a poem in which I am to figure. I am a farce and play to him, but to me this is all dreary reality. He takes all the profit and I bear all the burden.

CHAPTER ELEVEN

It is a strange circumstance, but it often occurs, that blessings by their use turn to curses—and that I, who in solitude, had desired sympathy as the only relief I could enjoy, should now find it an additional torture to me. During my father's lifetime I had always been of an affectionate and forbearing disposition, but since those days of joy, alas! I was much changed. I had become arrogant, peevish, and above all suspicious. Although the real interest of my narration is now ended and I ought quickly to wind up its melancholy catastrophe, yet I will relate one instance of my sad suspicious and despair—and how Woodville with the goodness and almost the power of an angel, softened my rugged feelings and led me back to gentleness.

He had promised to spend some hours with me one afternoon, but a violent and continual rain prevented him. I was alone the whole evening. I had passed two whole years alone unrepining, but now I was miserable. He could not really care for me, I thought, for, if he did, the storm would rather have made him come even if I had not expected him, than, as it did, prevent a promised visit. He would well know that this drear sky and gloomy rain would load my spirit almost to madness. If the weather had been fine, I should not have regretted his absence as heavily, as I necessarily must shut up in this miserable cottage with no companions but my own wretched thoughts. If he were truly my friend, he would have calculated all this—and let me now calculate this boasted friendship, and discover its real worth. He got over his grief for Elinor, and the country became dull to him—so he was glad to find even me for amusement. And when he does not know what else to do, he passes his lazy hours here, and calls this friendship. It is true that his presence is a consolation to me, and that his words are sweet, and, when he will, he can pour forth thoughts that win me from despair.

His words are sweet, and so, truly, is the honey of the bee, but the bee has a sting, and unkindness is a worse smart than that received from an insect's venom. I will put him to the proof. He says all hope is dead to him, and I know that it is dead to me. So, we are both equally fitted for death. Let me try if he will die with me. And, as I fear to die alone, if he will accompany me to cheer me—and thus, he can show himself my friend in the only manner my misery will permit.

It was madness, I believe, but I so worked myself up to this idea that I could think of nothing else. If he dies with me, it is well, and there will be an end of two miserable beings—and if he will not, then I will scoff at his friendship, and drink the poison before him to shame his cowardice.

I planned the whole scene with an earnest heart, and frantically set my soul on this project. I procured laundanum and, placing it in two glasses on the table, filled my room with flowers and decorated the last scene of my tragedy with the nicest care. As the hour for his coming approached, my heart softened and I wept—not that I gave up my plan, but, even when resolved, the mind must undergo several revolutions of feeling before it can drink its death.

Now all was ready, and Woodville came.

I received him at the door of my cottage and, leading him solemnly into the room, I said, "My friend, I wish to die. I am quite weary of enduring the misery which hourly I do endure, and I will throw it off. What slave will not, if he may, escape from his chains? Look, I weep. For more than two years, I have never enjoyed one moment free from anguish. I have often desired to die; but I am a very coward. It is hard for one so young, who was once so happy as I was, to voluntarily divest themselves of all sensation and to go alone to the dreary grave; I dare not. I must die, yet my fear chills me. I pause and shudder, and then for months I endure my excess of wretchedness. But now the time is come when I may quit life. I have a friend who will not refuse to accompany me in this dark journey. Such is my request: earnestly I do entreat and implore you to die with me. Then we shall find Elinor and what I have lost. Look, I am prepared; there is the death draft. Let us drink it together, and willingly and joyfully quit this hated round of daily life.

"You turn from me—yet, before you deny me, reflect, Woodville, how sweet it were to cast off the load of tears and misery under which we now labor. And surely we shall find light after we have passed the dark valley. That drink will plunge us into a sweet slumber, and when we awaken what joy will be ours to find all our sorrows and fears past. A little patience, and all will be over—aye, a very little patience. For, look, there is the key of our prison; we hold it in our own hands. Are we more debased than slaves to cast it away, and give ourselves up to voluntary bondage?

"Even now, if we had courage, we might be free. Behold, my cheek is flushed with pleasure at the imagination of death; all that we love are dead. Come, give me your hand—one look of joyous sympathy and we will go together and seek them; a lulling journey, where our arrival will bring bliss and our waking be that of angels.

"Do you delay? Are you a coward, Woodville? Oh fie! Cast off this blank look of human melancholy. Oh! That I had words to express the luxury of death that I might win you. I tell you we are no longer miserable mortals; we are about to become gods; spirits free and happy as gods. What fool on a bleak shore, seeing a flowery isle on the other side with his lost love beckoning to him from it, would pause because the wave is dark and turbid?

> What if some little payne the passage have
> That makes frayle flesh to fear the bitter wave?
> Is not short payne well borne that brings long ease,
> And lays the soul to sleep in quiet grave?

"Do you mark my words—I have learned the language of despair. I have it all by heart, for I am Despair—and a strange being am I, joyous, triumphant Despair. But those words are false, for a wave may be dark, but it is not bitter. We lie down, and close our eyes with a gentle goodnight, and when we wake, we are free. Come then, no more delay, you tardy one! Behold the pleasant potion! Look, I am a spirit of good, and not a human maid that invites you, and with winning accents (oh, that they would win you!) says, Come and drink."

As I spoke, I fixed my eyes upon his face—and his exquisite beauty, the heavenly compassion that beamed from his eyes, his gentle yet earnest look of deprecation and wonder even before he spoke—wrought a change in my high-strained feelings, taking from me all the sternness of despair and filling me only with the softest grief. I saw his eyes human also as he took both my hands in his; and sitting down near me, he said:

"This is a sad deed to which you would lead me, dearest friend, and your woe must indeed be deep that could fill you with these unhappy thoughts. You long for death—and yet you fear it and wish me to be your companion. But I have less courage than you and, even thus accompanied, I dare not die. Listen to me, and then reflect if you ought to win me to your project, even if, with the overbearing eloquence of despair, you could make black death so inviting that the fair heaven should appear darkness. Listen, I entreat you, to the words of one who has himself nurtured desperate thoughts, and longed with impatient desire for death—but who has at length trampled the phantom under foot, and crushed its sting. Come, as you have played Despair with me, I will play the part of Una with you and bring you hurtless from his dark cavern. Listen to me, and let yourself be softened by words, in which no selfish passion lingers.

"We know not what all this wide world means—its strange mixture of good and evil. But we have been placed here and bidden to live and hope. I know not what we are to hope, but there is some good beyond us that we must seek—and that is our Earthly task. If misfortune come against us, we must fight with it; we must cast it aside, and still go on to find out that which it is our nature to desire. Whether this prospect of future good be the preparation for another existence I know not. Or whether that it is merely that we, as workers in God's vineyard, must lend a hand to smooth the way for our posterity. If it indeed be that—if the efforts of the virtuous now, are to make the future inhabitants of this fair world more happy—if the labors of those who cast aside selfishness, and try to know the truth of things, are to free the people of ages now far distant, but which will one day come, from the burden under which those who now live groan, and, like you, weep bitterly—if they free them from but one of what are now the necessary evils of life—truly I will not fail, but will, with my whole soul, aid the work. From my youth I have said I will be virtuous; I will dedicate my life for the good of others; I will do my best to extirpate evil—and if the spirit who protects ill should so influence circumstances that I should suffer through my endeavor, yet while there is hope—and hope there ever must be—of success, cheerfully do I gird myself to my task.

"I have powers; others think well of them. Do you think I sow my seed in the barren air, and have no end in what I do? Believe me, I will never desert life until this last hope is torn from my heart—that in some way my labors may form a link in the chain of gold with which we ought all to strive to drag Happiness from where it sits enthroned above the clouds, now far beyond our reach, to inhabit the Earth with us.

"Let us suppose that Socrates, or Shakespeare, or Rousseau had been seized with despair and died in youth when they were as young as I am. Do you think that we and all the world should not have lost incalculable improvement in our good feelings and our happiness through their destruction? I am not like one of these; they influenced millions. But if I can influence but a hundred, but ten, but one solitary individual, so as in any way to lead him or her to good, that will be a joy to repay me for all my sufferings, though they were a million times multiplied—and that hope will support me to bear them.

"And those who do not work for posterity; or working, as may be my case, will not be known by it—yet they, believe me, have also their duties. You grieve because you are unhappy; it is happiness you seek, but you despair of obtaining it. But if you can bestow happiness on another—if you can give one other person only one hour of joy—ought you not to live to do it? And everyone has it in their power to do that. The inhabitants of this world suffer so much pain. In crowded cities, among cultivated plains, or on the desert mountains, pain is thickly sown—and if we can tear up but one of these noxious weeds, or more—if in its stead we can sow one seed of corn, or plant one fair flower, let that be motive sufficient against suicide. Let us not desert our task while there is the slightest hope that we may, in a future day, do this.

"Indeed, I dare not die. I have a mother whose support and hope I am. I have a friend who loves me as his life, and in whose breast I should enfix a mortal sting if I ungratefully left him. So I will not die. Nor shall you, my friend. Cheer up; cease to weep, I entreat you. Are you not young, and fair, and good? Why should you despair? Or, if you must for yourself, why for others? If you can never be happy, can you never bestow happiness? Oh, believe me, if you behold on my lips, pale with grief, one smile of joy and gratitude—and knew that you were parent of that smile, and that, without you, it had never been, you would feel so pure and warm a happiness that you would wish to live forever, again and again, to enjoy the same pleasure.

"Come, I see that you have already cast aside the sad thought you before frantically indulged. Look in that mirror; when I came, your brow was contracted, your eyes deep sunk in your head, your lips quivering. Your hands trembled violently when I took them, but now all is tranquil and soft. You are grieved, and there is grief in the expression of your countenance, but it is gentle and sweet. You allow me to throw away this cursed drink. You smile—oh, congratulate me, hope is triumphant, and I have done some good."

These words are shadowy as I repeat them but they were indeed words of fire, and produced a warm hope in me (I, miserable wretch, to hope!) that tingled like pleasure in my veins. He did not leave me for many hours; not until he had improved the spark that he had kindled, and with an angelic hand fostered the return of something that seemed like joy. He left me, but I still was calm—and, after I had saluted the starry sky and dewy earth with eyes of love and a contented goodnight, I slept sweetly, visited by dreams, the first of pleasure I had had for many long months.

But this was only a momentary relief, and my old habits of feeling returned, for I was doomed, while in life, to grieve. And to the natural sorrow of my father's death and its most terrific cause, imagination added a tenfold weight of woe. I believed myself to be polluted by the unnatural love I had inspired, and that I was a creature cursed and set apart by nature. I thought that, like another Cain, I had a mark set on my forehead to show humankind that there was a barrier between me and them. Woodville had told me that there was, in my face, an expression as if I belonged to another world. So he had seen that sign— and there it lay, a gloomy mark to tell the world that there was that within my soul that no silence could render sufficiently obscure.

Why, when fate drove me to become this outcast from human feeling; this monster with whom none might mingle in converse and love—why had she not, from that fatal and most accursed moment, shrouded me in thick mists and placed real darkness between me and my fellows, so that I might never more be seen? —and as I passed, like a murky cloud loaded with blight, they might only perceive me by the cold chill I should cast upon them, telling them, how truly, that something unholy was near? Then I should have lived upon this dreary heath unvisited, blasting none by my unhallowed gaze. Alas! I verily believe that, if the near prospect of death did not dull and soften my bitter feelings, if for a few months longer I had continued to live as I then lived—strong in body, but my soul corrupted to its core by a deadly cancer, if day after day I had dwelt on these dreadful sentiments—I should have become mad, and should have fancied myself a living pestilence. So horrible to my own solitary thoughts did this form, this voice, and all this wretched self appear, for had it not been the source of guilt that wants a name?

This was superstition. I did not feel thus frantically when

first I knew the holy name of father was become a curse to me. But my lonely life inspired me with wild thoughts. And then, when I saw Woodville, and day after day he tried to win my confidence and I never dared give words to my dark tale, I was impressed more strongly with the withering fear that I was in truth a marked creature, a pariah, only fit for death.

CHAPTER TWELVE

As I was perpetually haunted by these ideas, you may imagine that the influence of Woodville's words was very temporary; and that, although I did not again accuse him of unkindness, yet I soon became as unhappy as before.

Soon after this incident we parted. He heard that his mother was ill, and he hastened to her. He came to take leave of me, and we walked together on the heath for the last time. He promised that he would come and see me again, and bade me take cheer, and to encourage what happy thoughts I could, until time and fortitude should overcome my misery, and I could again mingle in society.

"Above all other admonition on my part," he said, "cherish and follow this one: Do not despair. That is the most dangerous gulf on which you perpetually totter, but you must reassure your steps, and take hope to guide you. Hope, and your wounds will be already half healed. But if you obstinately despair, there never more will be comfort for you. Believe me, my dearest friend, that there is a joy that the Sun and Earth and all its beauties can bestow that you will one day feel. The refreshing bliss of Love will again visit your heart, and undo the spell that binds you to woe, until you wonder how your eyes could be closed in the long night that burdens you.

"I dare not hope that I have inspired you with sufficient interest that the thought of me, and the affection that I shall ever bear you, will soften your melancholy and decrease the bitterness of your tears. But if my friendship can make you look on life with less disgust, beware how you injure it with suspicion. Love is a delicate sprite, and easily hurt by rough jealousy. Guard, I entreat you, a firm persuasion of my sincerity in the inmost recesses of your heart, out of the reach of the casual winds that may disturb its surface. Your temper is made unequal by suffering, and the tenor of your mind is, I fear, sometimes shaken by unworthy causes—but let your confidence in my sympathy and love be deeper far, and incapable of being reached by these agitations that come and go, and, if they touch not, your affections leave you uninjured."

These were some of Woodville's last lessons. I wept as I listened to him, and, after we had taken an affectionate farewell, I followed him far with my eyes until they saw the last of my Earthly comforter. I had insisted on accompanying him across the heath towards the town where he dwelt. The sun was yet high when he left me, and I turned my steps towards my cottage. It was at the latter end of the month of September when the nights have become chill. But the weather was serene, and, as I walked on, I fell into no unpleasing reveries. I thought of Woodville with gratitude and kindness and did not, I know not why, regret his departure with any bitterness. It seemed that, after one great shock, all other change was trivial to me; and I walked on wondering when the time would come when we should, all four, with my dearest father restored to me, meet in some sweet Paradise. I pictured to myself a lovely river such as that on whose banks Dante describes Matilda gathering flowers, whichever flows…

> —bruna, bruna
> Sotto l'ombra perpetua, che mai
> Raggiar non lascia sole ivi, nè Luna.

> brown, brown
> under an eternal shadow, which forbids
> a single ray from Sun or Moon

…and then I repeated to myself all that lovely passage that relates the entrance of Dante into the terrestrial Paradise; and thought it would be sweet when I wandered on those lovely banks to see the car of light descend with my long lost parent to be restored to me. As I waited there in expectation of that moment, I thought how, of the lovely flowers that grew there, I would wind myself a chaplet and crown myself for joy. I would sing *sul margine d'un rio*, my father's favorite song, and that my voice gliding through the windless air would announce to him, in whatever bower he sat expecting the moment of our union, that his daughter was come. Then the mark of misery would have faded from my brow, and I should raise my eyes fearlessly to meet his, which ever beamed with the soft luster of innocent love. When I reflected on the magic look of those deep eyes, I wept, but gently, lest my sobs should disturb the fairy scene.

I was so entirely wrapped in this reverie that I wandered on, taking no heed of my steps until I actually stooped down to gather a flower for my wreath on that bleak plain where no flower grew, when I awoke from my daydream and found myself I knew not where.

The Sun had set and the roseate hue which the clouds had caught from him in his descent had nearly died away. A wind swept across the plain. I looked around me and saw no object that told me where I was—I had lost myself, and in vain attempted to find my path. I wandered on, and the coming darkness made every trace indistinct by which I might be guided. At length all was veiled in the deep obscurity of blackest night. I became weary and, knowing that my servant was to sleep that night at the neighboring village, so that my absence would alarm no one; and that I was safe in this wild spot from every intruder, I resolved to spend the night where I was. Indeed, I was too weary to walk farther. The air was chill, but I was careless of bodily inconvenience, and I thought that I was well inured to the weather during my two years of solitude, when no change of seasons prevented my perpetual wanderings.

I lay upon the grass, surrounded by a darkness which not the slightest beam of light penetrated. There was no sound, for the deep night had laid to sleep the insects, the only creatures that lived on the lone spot where no tree or shrub could afford shelter to aught else. There was a wondrous silence in the air that calmed my senses yet which enlivened my soul, my mind hurried from image to image and seemed to grasp an eternity. All in my heart was shadowy yet calm, until my ideas became confused and at length died away in sleep.

When I awoke, it rained. I was already quite wet, and my limbs were stiff and my head giddy with the chill of night. It was a drizzling, penetrating shower. As my dank hair clung to my neck and partly covered my face, I had hardly strength to part with my fingers the long straight locks that fell before my eyes. The darkness was much dissipated and in the east where the clouds were least dense, the moon was visible behind the thin grey cloud—

> The moon is behind, and at the full
> And yet she looks both small and dull.

Its presence gave me a hope that by its means I might find my home. But I was languid, and many hours passed before I could reach the cottage, dragging as I did my slow steps, and often resting on the wet earth, unable to proceed.

I particularly mark this night, for it was that which has hurried on the last scene of my tragedy, which else might have dwindled on through long years of listless sorrow. I was very ill when I arrived and quite incapable of taking off my wet clothes that hung about me. In the morning, on her return, my servant found me almost lifeless—while possessed by a high fever, I was lying on the floor of my room.

I was very ill for a long time, and when I recovered from the immediate danger of fever, every symptom of a rapid consumption declared itself. I was for some time ignorant of this and thought that my excessive weakness was the consequence of the fever. But my strength became less and less; as winter came on, I had a cough; and my sunken cheek, before pale, burned with a hectic fever. One by one these symptoms struck me, and I became convinced that the moment I had so much desired was about to arrive and that I was dying. I was sitting by my fire, the physician who had attended me ever since my fever, had just left me, and I looked over his prescription in which digitalis was the prominent medicine.

"Yes," I said, "I see how this is, and it is strange that I should have deceived myself so long. I am about to die an innocent death, and it will be sweeter even than that which the opium promised."

I rose and walked slowly to the window; the wide heath was covered by snow, which sparkled under the beams of the sun that shone brightly through the pure, frosty air. A few birds were pecking some crumbs under my window. I smiled with quiet joy; and in my thoughts, which through long habit would forever connect themselves into one train, as if I shaped them into words, I thus addressed the scene before me:

> Rolled round in Earth's diurnal course
> With rocks, and stones, and trees.

"For it will be the same with You, who are called our Universal Mother, when I am gone. I have loved you; and in my days, both of happiness and sorrow, I have peopled your solitudes with wild fancies of my own creation. The woods, and lakes, and mountains which I have loved, have for me a thousand associations; and you, oh, Sun! have smiled upon—and borne your part in—many imaginations that sprung to life in my soul alone, and which will die with me. Your solitudes, sweet land, your trees and waters will still exist, moved by your winds, or still beneath the eye of noon, though what I have felt about you, and all my dreams which have often strangely deformed you, will die with me. You will exist to reflect other images in other minds, and ever will remain the same, although your reflected semblance vary in a thousand ways, changeable as the hearts of those who view you. One of these fragile mirrors, that ever doted on your image, is about to be broken, crumbled to dust. But ever-teeming Nature will create another and another, and you will lose nought by my destruction.

"You will ever be the same. Receive then the grateful farewell of a fleeting shadow who is about to disappear, who joyfully leaves you, yet with a last look of affectionate thankfulness. Farewell! Sky, and fields and woods; the lovely flowers that grow on you; your mountains and your rivers. To the balmy air and the strong wind of the north, to all, a last farewell. I shall shed no more tears, for my task is almost fulfilled, and I am about to be rewarded for long and most burdensome suffering. Bless your child even in death, as I bless you. And let me sleep at peace in my quiet grave."

I feel death to be near at hand and I am calm. I no longer despair, but look on all around me with placid affection. I find it sweet to watch the progressive decay of my strength, and to repeat to myself, another day and yet another, but again I shall not see the red leaves of autumn. Before that time, I shall be with my father.

I am glad Woodville is not with me, for perhaps he would grieve, and I desire to see smiles alone during the last scene of my life. When I last wrote to him, I told him of my ill health— but not of its mortal tendency, lest he should conceive it to be his duty to come to me, for I fear lest the tears of friendship should destroy the blessed calm of my mind. I take pleasure in arranging all the little details which will occur when I shall no longer be.

In truth I am in love with death; no maiden ever took more pleasure in the contemplation of her bridal attire than I in fancying my limbs already enwrapped in their shroud. Is it not my marriage dress? Alone, it will unite me to my father when, in an eternal mental union, we shall never part.

I will not dwell on the last changes that I feel in the final decay of nature. It is rapid but without pain. I feel a strange pleasure in it. For long years these are the first days of peace that have visited me. I no longer exhaust my miserable heart by bitter tears and frantic complaints; I no longer reproach the Sun, the Earth, the air, for pain and wretchedness. I wait in quiet expectation for the closing hours of a life which has been to me most sweet and bitter. I do not die not having enjoyed life—for sixteen years I was happy. During the first months of my father's return, I had enjoyed ages of pleasure. Now indeed I am grown old in grief; my steps are feeble like those of age.I have become peevish and unfit for life; so, having passed little more than twenty years upon the Earth I am more fit for my narrow grave than many are when they reach the natural term of their lives.

Again and again I have passed over in my remembrance the different scenes of my short life. If the world is a stage and I merely an actor on it, my part has been strange, and, alas! tragical. Almost from infancy, I was deprived of all the testimonies of affection which children generally receive. I was thrown entirely upon my own resources, and I enjoyed what I may almost call unnatural pleasures, for they were dreams and not realities. The Earth was to me a magic lantern and I a gazer, and a listener but no actor.

But then came the transporting and soul-reviving era of my existence—my father returned, and I could pour my warm affections on a human heart; there was a new Sun and a new Earth created to me; the waters of existence sparkled. Joy! joy! but, alas! what grief! My bliss was more rapid than the progress of a sunbeam on a mountain, which discloses its glades and woods, and then leaves it dark and blank. To my happiness followed madness and agony, closed by despair.

This was the drama of my life which I have now depicted upon paper. During three months I have been employed in this task. The memory of sorrow has brought tears; the memory of happiness a warm glow, the lively shadow of that joy. Now my tears are dried, the glow has faded from my cheeks, and with a few words of farewell to you, Woodville, I close my work—the last that I shall perform.

Farewell, my only living friend. You are the sole tie that binds me to existence, and now I break it. It gives me no pain to leave you, nor can our separation give you much. You never regarded me as one of this world, but rather as a being who, for some penance, was sent from the Kingdom of Shadows. And she passed a few days weeping on the earth and longing to return to her native soil. You will weep, but they will be tears of gentleness. I would, if I thought that it would lessen your regret, tell you to smile and congratulate me on my departure from the misery you beheld me endure. I would say: "Woodville, rejoice with your friend, I triumph now and am most happy." But I check these expressions; these may not be the consolations of the living; they weep for their own misery, and not for that of the being they have lost. No, shed a few natural tears due to my memory—and if you ever visit my grave, pluck from there a flower, and lay it to your heart; for your heart is the only tomb in which my memory will be entered.

My death is rapidly approaching, and you are not near to watch the flitting and vanishing of my spirit. Do not regret this, for death is a too terrible an object for the living. It is one of those adversities which hurt instead of purifying the heart, for it is so intense a misery that it hardens and dulls the feelings. Dreadful as the time was, when I pursued my father towards the ocean, and found there only his lifeless corpse, yet for my own sake I should prefer that to the watching, one by one, his senses fade; his pulse weaken—and sleeplessly, as it were devour his life in gazing. To see life in his limbs and to know that soon life would no longer be there, to see the warm breath issue from his lips and to know they would soon be chill—I will not continue to trace this frightful picture. You suffered this torture once; I never did. And the remembrance fills your heart sometimes with bitter despair, when otherwise your feelings would have melted into soft sorrow.

So, day by day, I become weaker, and life flickers in my wasting form, as a lamp about to lose its vivifying oil. I'm now behind the glad sun of May. It was May, four years ago, that I first saw my beloved father; it was in May, three years ago that my folly destroyed the only being I was doomed to love. May is returned, and I die.

Three days ago, the anniversary of our meeting, and, alas! of our eternal separation, after a day of killing emotion, I caused myself to be led once more to behold the face of nature. I caused myself to be carried to some meadows some miles distant from my cottage. The grass was being mowed, and there was the scent of hay in the fields; all the Earth looked fresh, and its inhabitants happy. Evening approached and I beheld the sun set. Three years ago, and on that day and hour, it shone through the branches and leaves of the beech wood and its beams flickered upon the face of him whom I then beheld for the last time. I now saw that divine orb, gilding all the clouds with unwonted splendor, sink behind the horizon. It disappeared from a world where he whom I would seek exists not; it approached a world where he exists not.

Why do I weep so bitterly? Why does my heart heave with vain endeavor to cast aside the bitter anguish that covers it "as the water covers the sea." I go from this world, where he is no longer, and soon I shall meet him in another.

Farewell, Woodville, the turf will soon be green on my grave; and the violets will bloom on it. There is my hope and my expectation. Yours are in this world; may they be fulfilled.

NOTES

As Mary Shelley's manuscript had not reached a proper publisher or editor in her lifetime, the text required significant editing. Her writing style, perhaps appropriate for someone in emotional distress, tended toward breathlessness with run-on sentences, parenthetical interjections, oh-by-the-ways, inconsistent or missing punctuation. The goal of this edition has been to achieve straightforward readability for the modern reader. Consequently, editing has been applied for punctuation, obvious slip-ups in the text, substitution of "you" for "thee" or "ye," and, as unobtrusively as possible, making sentences out of half-sentences or fragments.

Unfamiliar words and references are listed below; in the ebook edition, the text is interactive, with unmarked links from text to notes. My translations of quotations have been added to the text; an educated reader in her day may have been familiar with Dante in the Italian, but most of us today are not.

Adam : the first man, in the Hebrew Testament, who shared an apple with Eve, and was banished.

Alfieri : Count Vittorio Alfieri, playwright and playboy

Anchises : father of Aeneas by Aphrodite (Venus); struck blind for revealing their affair

as a rainbow gleams : as a rainbow gleams upon a cataract, to soften thy tremendous sorrows. —Byron, Childe Harold

Beatrice : Beatrice Portinari, a woman whom Dante adored; though she died young and married to someone else, Dante employed her in his *Divina Commedia* as his guide to Paradise.

Better have loved despair : Better have loved despair, and safer kissed her. Possibly a reference to Tennyson's: 'Tis better to have loved and lost: Than never to have loved at all

Before I see another day : Before I see another day
   Oh, let this body die away! —*Wordsworth*

Boccaccio : Giovanni Boccaccio, Italian author of the *Decameron*.

bruna, bruna : bruna bruna
   Sotto l'ombra perpetua, che mai
   Raggiar non lascia sole ivi, nè Luna
      brown, brown
      under an eternal shadow, which forbids
      a single ray from Sun or Moon
         —Dante, *Purgatorio*

cavern of Antiparos : cave on a Greek island noted for its variety of stalactites and stalagmites.

chaplet : garland for the head; string of beads for prayer

Comus : a masque, or closet drama by John Milton

Constance : Queen in Shakespeare's *King John*. Also, possibly an unintentional word play ("change constance")

consumption : tuberculosis

cope : covering

David : shepherd boy who played the lyre for King Saul, and later became King himself.

dingle : a shady dell

Dr. Darwin : Erasmus Darwin, leading Enlightenment thinker and natural philosopher. Grandfather of Charles Darwin

E quasi mi perdei : E quasi mi perdei gli occhi chini—*Dante*

Eumenides : the Furies. Eumenides (the kindly ones) is a euphemism (misleading expression)

for what should I do here : —for what should I do here,
   Like a decaying flower, still withering
   Under his bitter words, whose kindly heat
   Should give my poor heart life?
      —Beaumont and Fletcher, *The Captain*

furze : gorse; low thorny evergreen shrubbery

Gli occhi drizzo : Gli occhi drizzo ver me con quel sembiante
Che madre fa sopra figlioul deliro — *Dante, Paradiso*

Job : Figure in the Hebrew Testament, subjected to many trials and difficulties for no other reason than to settle an argument between God and the Devil

magic lantern : a rotating lampshade with cutouts and silhouettes of figures that appear to dance on the wall, from the light of the lamp in a darkened room. The term was later applied to early motion pictures, which, with a powerful beam, projected light images on a screen.

mariner : hallucination of water snakes, from Samuel Taylor Coleridge's *Rime of the Ancient Mariner.*

Matilda gathering flowers : In *Purgatorio*, Dante meets Matilda, a women gathering flowers by a river.

Medusa : a beautiful woman turned into a creature. Any human to look on her turned to stone; her hair was snakes.

miniature : pocket-sized portrait, sometimes encased in a locket

Miranda : character in Shakespeare's *The Tempest*

moon is behind : The moon is behind, and at the full
And yet she looks both small and dull.
— Samuel Taylor Coleridge, Christabel

Noujahad : The History of Noujahad, a popular Eastern tale published in 1792, written by Mrs. F. Sheridan

Oedipus : tragic Greek King, whose destiny was prophesied

Ond' era pinta : Ond' era pinta tutta la mia via—*Dante*

plain of Enna : highland in Sicily

post chaise : fast carriage for mail and a few passengers.

Prometheus : Titan who shared the gift of fire with humankind, and was punished for doing so.

Proserpine : also known as Persephone, daughter of Ceres

Psyche : a princess who loves a god, and, after difficult trials, she is allowed to marry Cupid/Eros.

public school : in Britain, "public school" means fee-based elite private school

rill : small brook, rivulet

Rolled round in Earth's :
> Rolled round in Earth's diurnal course
> With rocks, and stones, and trees.
> — Wordsworth

Rosalind : lead character in Shakespeare's *As You Like It*

seven sleepers : the Seven Sleepers of Ephesus. A legend that seven men were condemned by a campaign against Christians, when found sleeping in a cave, the cave was sealed. When they emerged, thinking it was one day, they found that two hundred years had passed, and the kingdom had become Christian while they slept.

Sigismunda mourning over the heart of Guiscardo : painting by William Hogarth, based on a story by Boccaccio

simoon : hot Saharan wind

Spenser : Edmund Spenser, a medievalist writer. His most famous work is the epic The Faerie Queene

Sul Margine D'un Rio (On the Bank of a River) **:** melody by Felix Horetzky

sylvan Hunter : Diana, goddess of the hunt

there were none to praise : —there were none to praise
And very few to love —*Wordsworth*

tartan rachan : a tartan was originally a woven pattern specific to a clan; rachan or rauchan is a shepherd's wrap.

water snakes to the bewitched mariner : reference to Samuel Taylor Coleridge's *Rime of the Ancient Mariner*

What if some little payne :
> What if some little payne the passage have
> That makes frayle flesh to fear the bitter wave?
> Is not short payne well borne that brings long ease,
> And lays the soul to sleep in quiet grave?
> —Edmund Spenser, *Faerie Queene*

Una : a maiden in Edmund Spenser's *The Faerie Queene*

vacuity : emptiness

water covers the sea : reference in Habakkuk, *Hebrew Testament*

Where is now my hope? : Where is now my hope?
        For my hope who shall see it?
        They shall go down together to the bars of the pit,
        when our rest together is in the dust
                — Job, *Hebrew Testament*

Whispered so and so : Whispered so and so
        In dark hint soft and low
           —Samuel Taylor Coleridge

world is a stage : All the world's a stage…, a reference from William Shakespeare's *As You Like It*